MONTANA Promises

A Montana Romance

MONTANA Promises

A Montana Romance

VELDA
BROTHERTON

GALWAY

OGHMA CREATIVE MEDIA

www.oghmacreative.com

ISBN: 978-1-63373-089-2

Interior Design by Elizabeth Easter
Editing by Gil Miller

Galway Press
Oghma Creative Media
Bentonville, Arkansas
www.oghmacreative.com

To my husband, Don, with love

A special thanks to Dusty Richards and Lisa Wingate,
and the gang at Northwest Arkansas Writers' Workshop.
Without your help it would never have happened.

Foreword

This book originally was my very first publication. Intending it to be a western, I was told by a western editor that it needed to be turned into a romance because of the female protagonist. So that's what I did, and it came out from Topaz in 1994.

The publication happened so quickly I walked around in a daze for months. In fact, it was chosen at the last minute when another author failed to meet her deadline and a space opened up. The manuscript was lying on my editor's desk; she'd read it once as a romance. The original cover was computer-generated. It featured Steve Sandalis, the Topaz Man. I would later meet him at a *Romantic Times* Conference. He was a bit shy and very charming.

Attending that first conference was a culture shock, but I recovered nicely.

My editor told me later that I'd kept my hero and heroine apart for too much of the book, and I wasn't to do it again. We laughed about that later, but I was more careful with the books that followed. I was accustomed to writing westerns, and turning one into a romance challenged me. I still feel my books are more western than romances.

We are told, as authors, to write what we know. I disagree with that. I say, write about what we want to know. And that's what I did when I wrote this series that takes place in the Big Sky country of Montana. All my life I'd wanted to go to Montana. My Dad would go hunting in Wyoming and Montana once every year and I'd beg him to let me go along. But in those days, girls didn't do such manly things. Once I began this series, I visited Montana every day in my research, and later the actual writing. I dug deeply into Montana's culture, the flora and fauna of the countryside, and traveled from one small town to another.

One day after a couple of the books were published, I was pleased to receive a phone call from a lady in California who said she was raised in Montana and when she read my books she felt as if she'd gone home. I couldn't have received better praise.

Several years later, I was able to visit Montana and Wyoming, and when we went to the preserved ghost town of Virginia City, felt as if I were going home myself. I knew this place, where Reed and Tressie spent so much time. The cover of this book is an actual photograph of Virginia City, Montana.

If you enjoy my books, I'd be pleased if you would write a review at Amazon.

I can be reached at *www.veldabrotherton.com.*

One

Tressie smoothed the mound of the double grave with the back of a shovel. A burning southwest wind licked at the tears and sweat on her cheeks. Weary with grief and exhausted from chopping at the hard earth, she sagged against the wooden handle and gazed at the small plot of disturbed soil.

Anger overpowered sorrow, for she found it somehow easier to manage. The unspoken fury could be shouted at the endless white-hot sky, and she did just that, damning her father with long, anguished howls.

The eternal land swallowed her cries and fell silent. Across the arid and flat prairie, shades of dull brown spread like death as far as she could see in any direction.

She fisted the bib of her tattered overalls in folded hands, and lowering her head moved her lips in silence, hoping for a prayer to comfort the shattered remnants of her soul. But none came. Hope had withered and dried as the months passed with no word from her father.

After a long while she plodded back toward the soddy, dragging the shovel along behind. A stiff wind boosted her reluctant steps, snapping the coarse overalls against her legs. Carried on that wind came the distinct whicker of a horse. She stopped for a moment to scan the prairie, leaning on the shovel and shading her eyes against the brutal sun. Nothing but endless, wavering heat waves and burned grasses.

Oh, how she hated this terrible place. How she wished for someone, anyone, to come and take her away. There it was again; a soft blowing snort. There was a horse nearby.

Hauling up, she faced south, and spotted the lone rider. Man and horse appeared in the distance as if spewed from the earth itself. A familiar trick of the heat-scorched prairie, but a sight that never failed to startle her.

Shading her eyes with one hand, she studied the wavering image, afraid it was only another mirage. If real, who would it be? And where was he bound? Her heart pounded with a mix of excitement and fear. Was this simply a foolish prospector short of food and water?

After the gold strikes, men had poured across the plains like scatterings of lost cattle, some passing on by, others stopping to water at the well in the yard. At first she had been frightened by the strangers, but soon realized that they had but one thing on their minds. GOLD. GOLD. GOLD. It was like a wild disease with them, and one Papa soon caught. Surely there wouldn't be enough of the precious ore to go around.

Once assured that the horse and rider headed straight for her were not a figment of her imagination, she whirled and ran for the house. At the unprotected doorway she tossed down the shovel and scurried inside. From the gloomy corner she lifted a long, heavy Kentucky rifle. Just in case this traveler had more than gold on his mind, she thumbed the hammer to half cock and fingered a percussion cap from the fireplace mantel. She had fired the gun off two days ago and reloaded it, just as Papa had taught her to do.

"Keep the powder dry and keep her loaded all but for the cap," he'd warned. With steady fingers she placed the cap on the nipple and waited.

Outside, the rhythmic thud of the horse's hooves ceased. She held her breath and didn't move, but nothing happened. Except for the wind, no sound. She peered from the open doorway. The dusty rear haunches and tail of a bony sorrel protruded from around the corner. Nothing stirred save a flick of the matted tail.

What was the man doing hiding out back there? And why didn't he climb down or hail the house?

She crept a few steps into the sunny yard and hefted the gun barrel to aim at something but the ground.

"What do you want?" The question came out like a squawk and she tried to work saliva down her dry throat.

No answer. She took a few more steps, the clumsy shoes scuffing up puffs of dust.

Scorching air hung heavy with the odor of horse and sweat, and something she couldn't identify. A brackish, overpowering stench that made her remember the smell in the house before she had removed the birthing bed and burned it.

Inching past the corner of the house, she made out a figure slumped forward in the saddle, not moving. She halted and swallowed harshly. It was blood she smelled. Too much blood.

Maybe death, too, lurking just around that corner. Terror took her heart in its fist and she gasped for air past a gagging nausea. Despite all her heartache and loneliness, she did not want to face death. Not some stranger's, and certainly not her own. She'd been up all night with Mama's vain struggles to bear the child. She staggered against the hardened sod bricks of the cabin to keep from going to her knees.

A prayer came to her then, as it wouldn't earlier over the grave. It was only a simple plea for help, and she offered the words up with little hope they would be heard. She asked for just enough strength to see her through one more hardship. Goodness knows, there'd been plenty of those in her seventeen years.

Gasping in a breath, she spread her long legs and once more lifted the heavy rifle to sight on the rumpled shirt of the stranger. "Stay right where you are." The steadiness of the tone amazed her.

"I don't think I have much choice," came a feeble reply. The voice, though cracked by weariness, held an edge of determination. "I could use a hand here. I'd surely hate to fall off this horse, but I reckon it's about to happen."

Expelling a breath of relief, she leaned the gun against the house. There wasn't enough punch left in this fellow to hurt a rabbit, let alone her. Though she was a strapping young woman, the man almost knocked her to her knees when he slid from the saddle into the support of her arms. For a while she thought they wouldn't make it inside. A couple of times she had to stop and rest, and he wasn't doing a whole lot to help her, either. He did drag one leg after the other, but for the most part she supported his weight. He groaned with each step. Head tucked under his arm, the gamy smell of his body nearly overpowered her. He must have been on the trail a long time without benefit of a good washing.

The corn-shuck bed in one corner of the single room appeared miles away, but she got him there. Letting the limp body sprawl where it fell, she ignored his pitiful moans. Exhausted, she collapsed into the rocking chair between the fireplace and the bed. It was Mama's chair and the only one they had managed to bring with them from Missouri. Resting there was the nearest she could come to the solace of her dear dead mother's arms.

It didn't take long for the aroma of cooking food to revive her. She'd set a pot of soup on the fire early that morning before Mama's birthing pains had grown so intense that all Tressie could do was tend her. She hadn't had a bite to eat since the night before. With scarcely enough energy to crawl, she made her way to the soup pot and ladled out a bowlful, sank to the floor and drank the thin broth, relishing the few chunks of potato, cabbage, and squash.

"I wonder if I could have a sip of that?" The man on the bed whispered.

She filled the bowl again and reached it up to him. He managed to raise his head and grasp the bowl in one hand, but then was unable to put it to his lips. Lowering his mouth, he tried to lap at the soup like a dog. She came to her knees and shakily tipped the rim to his mouth so he could drink. Broth dribbled down his darkly-stubbled chin, but he managed to swallow some.

"We're a fine pair," she said. "Can't hardly tell which one is the worse off for our troubles."

He noisily sucked up the last drop and let out a feeble sigh before his head lolled back onto the bed. From the rhythm of his breathing he had either fallen asleep or was unconscious. Dried blood caked one side of his shirt. She could do nothing for him until she got some rest, and that was all there was to that. He would either have to lie there and die in poor Mama's clean bed or hold out until she awoke.

Before giving in to her own weariness, she fetched the rifle from outside. Removing the percussion cap, she eased the hammer down and stood the precious weapon back in its place. Every muscle in her body quivered, begging for rest. At last she succumbed, stretching out on a pallet on the earthen floor, where she immediately fell asleep.

A narrow slant of morning sun crept through the window to lie warmly on her cheek. Fear gripped her when she caught sight of the man on the bed before she recalled his arrival the previous day. He could have recovered enough to have had his way with her while she lay nearly unconscious on the floor. She immediately dismissed the thought as tomfoolery, considering his condition. A touch to his brow told her he had not died overnight, though he was burning with fever. Probably from the wound in his shoulder.

For a moment she left her hand lying there to study his features. Gaunt as he was, there was a savage grace about the shape of him. High cheekbones brushed by long dark lashes, prominent nose, a good sturdy brow. The hair, though dusty with travel, was long and black as a raven's wing. Washed, it would reflect the blue-purple shimmer of true ebony. Some Indian blood there.

He stirred and she jerked her hand away, afraid he would awaken and find her staring. But he only shifted an arm so that it lay across his chest. Though grimy, his nails were trimmed, the fingers long and calloused. Thank goodness he hadn't died during the night, leaving her another body to deal with. He might well be more of a problem alive, though.

Taking up the water bucket, she went outdoors into the pearlescent dawn. A breeze freshened into gusts, whipping up spirals of dust devils that settled in a fine grit on her skin. At the well she stripped out of the stiff overalls and bathed from a bucket of cold water, using a bar of yucca-root soap to lather her short hair. The morning sun would dry it quickly, bringing out the red highlights she had once been so proud of. Oh how angry Papa was when she chopped the waist-long tresses off during the backbreaking labor of that first summer they spent on the hot, windy plains. Never mind the only water they had at the time was hauled several miles in wooden barrels, he still wanted to keep his long-haired, winsome little girl. Papa had always been unrealistic in his expectations of everything life had to offer.

After the family had been there awhile, a drifter helped them dig the well in return for food from their summer garden. Though everyone was grateful, the man's tales of gold strikes in Oregon Territory soon convinced Papa to abandon the farm and renew his quest for easy fortune, this time alone. The gold camps were no place for the burden of a family, he explained to his tearful wife and daughter.

Papa. Oh, Papa, just see what you did.

A tear slid from one eye. She slung it away with an angry swipe.

She drew another bucket of water and poured it over her head. The icy embrace drove away the last remnants of sleep, and she turned into the wind and closed her eyes.

The loss of her mother and the boy-child who had slipped from Mama's womb without uttering even one feeble cry overwhelmed her. Her heart swelled into a huge aching knot. She wanted to go home. Desperately missed the green Missouri hills and the thick forests and hidden streams. How she hated this unbroken, wind-tossed land.

What nonsense. If she were to survive, there was no time for grief or such useless longings. Just as well to put the yesterdays behind her; they were over and done with. Everyone was gone: Mama and the young'un in their grave, Papa off and wandering, gone to seek his fortune. Dead, for all she knew. But best not admit yet to such a possibility. For if he was still alive, she would find him one day. And she would look him right in the eye and tell him how much she hated him for leaving Mama to die. Going off and deserting the ones who loved him, for what? Tales of gold.

Somewhere out across that flat prairie Papa wandered. She stood tall and pressed both hands into the small of her back, stretching, gazing into the endless expanse. And her, left here alone totally dependent upon herself for what happened for the rest of her life. It was certainly childish to go on believing in Papa's return, for that wasn't going to happen. The admission surprisingly strengthened her resolve. If he lived, the man inside might help get her out of this predicament, though she hated depending on anyone save herself.

Wiping water from her eyes, she caught sight of the horse the man had rode in on. The bony creature lay on the ground, feet stuck stiffly out to one side. The poor thing had fallen down dead during the night and she hadn't even heard it. She would have to get the saddle off and see what she could do about dragging the dead animal away from the soddy. Sure as anything, with this heat, the smell would soon attract hordes of flies and fill the cabin with a poisonous stench. A chunk of the meat would add taste to her normal fare of thin soup.

Squaring her bare shoulders, she drew another bucket of water, stepped over the pile of dirty clothes, and walked naked to the soddy. She spared no further thought for the dead sorrel. There was only so much a body could handle at one time, and she'd about reached her limit.

All caught up in newfound considerations of her aloneness, she had yet to wonder about the condition of the man lying in the bed over in the darkened corner. He would either live or die, and she would do all she could for him. That was that. She stepped inside and nearly dropped the bucket when he shouted out:

"All dead. All. God help us. I can't go on...I can't."

She recovered quickly. He was raving out of his head, probably didn't even know she was there. Who had shot him, and from who or what was he running? A half-breed Indian on the run could mean just about anything from a simple farm raid for food to a massacre, though his dress was that of a white man. Perhaps he'd been involved in a robbery or killing and was an outlaw. The possibilities were endless, and she would find out as soon as he was coherent. Heaven knew, she had no desire to shelter a killer.

First, she might ought to put on something. The one dress she could still call more than a rag was dreadfully threadbare, and Mama's were much too small. She lifted it off a hook in the corner and wiggled into the thin garment. Lean of shank, she'd look like a boy, were it not for her high, firm breasts. Once she might have taken more note of their maturation over the past year or so. Now it didn't really matter much. That the dress was stretched a bit too tight across the chest when she slipped it on barely caught her notice.

The man still slept and she had to keep him alive. He made puckery faces when she pulled the blood-stiffened shirt away to look at his shoulder. The wound wasn't as bad as she'd expected. The bullet appeared to have passed through the muscle without hitting the bone.

There'd been no bleeding overnight, but it did need a good cleaning, both front and back.

She cut away the rest of the shirt and drew in a ragged breath. He was skin and bones, his ribs standing out so you could count them. Most likely he had passed out from hunger as much as from the bullet wound. Poor creature. She smoothed a shag of damp hair back away from his cheek, felt the heat of fever. Dear God, would he die? The thought brought unbidden tears. There had been enough death in this little cabin for a while. The fear it might only end when she herself died froze her there for a moment, staring down at him.

The man needed a bath as badly as he needed anything, and she took the time to build a fire and heat plenty of water before cleaning and binding his wound. Granny always swore you couldn't even get over a runny nose if you weren't clean, and despite her situation, Tressie clung to that principle.

Steam from the water filled the small room. She lathered a rag and washed the bluish wound, perfectly round in the front where the ball had entered, gaping and ugly at the back where it had come out. She tried not to hurt him, but he groaned constantly until she finished. When at last the shoulder was bound in the remnants of one of her worn-out petticoats, the pitiful moaning ceased. He never opened his eyes, even when she undressed him and scoured the dirt from his painfully thin body. Hand supporting the knee of one long leg, she washed the grimy skin and tried not to notice that he was a man.

She was, after all, old enough to think of a man of her own, but the rawboned frontier life had presented no possibilities. Romance existed only in rare dreams that came only when she wasn't so exhausted she fell into a stupor at bedtime.

After completing the man's bath, she tucked a quilt around his shivering frame and lay a dampened cloth on his forehead. His fever had gone down some.

In the remainder of boiling water still in the pot on the coals, Tressie stirred up cornmeal mush. She was dipping the thick stuff into a bowl when he spoke in a dried and grating tone that startled her in its abruptness.

"I thought you were a vision and I had died."

She stood and took him the steaming bowl. "Well, I'm not and you didn't. Sorry, this is all I have. It's weevily, but filling."

He grabbed at the bowl, almost dumped its contents. She rescued it and offered the first spoonful, ashamed when he sucked air and rolled the steaming mush around in his mouth before swallowing.

"It's too hot," she said by way of apology, and began to blow on each bite before giving it to him. He gulped down mouthful after mouthful, pursing his lips for the next offering before she had it cooled.

To cover her discomfort at his pitiful condition, she began to chatter as she fed him. "If we were back on the farm in Missouri, there would be milk and sweet cream butter from the cow and molasses sorghum for sweetin' and flour for bread. Instead of this wearisome dry heat, there'd be damp cool mornings and long, lazy afternoons when a body could shell peas or snap beans or shuck corn out under the shade of a big old hickory and not even notice it was summer."

His eyes stared at the movements of her mouth but he didn't miss a beat in the feeding.

Caught up in memory, she could almost forget the dilemma

facing her and this stranger, and take his measure. His eyes, dark as bottomless caves, held a sadness that plucked at her. Since she d washed it his long black hair shimmered with shades of blue. The stubble of whiskers covering his square jaw looked more like he hadn't shaved in a while than like he might ordinarily wear a beard. She couldn't guess his age, though she guessed him several years older than herself. Somewhere between twenty-five and thirty.

Once begun, she couldn't stop the jabbering, but slowed down the feeding process to keep him from getting sick. "I just have to make do because the cow died last winter, the sorghum run out before that, and Papa took our only horse when he went off in search of his fortune, so we couldn't ride in for supplies if there was any money, which there isn't." She bit at her lip. Telling that small lie was just in case he was a thief and might get ideas when his strength came back.

Mama's few hoarded coins were well hidden.

"After the Preemption Act made squatting legal, Papa couldn't wait to leave Missouri and come out here. He talked about land that stretched as far as the eye could see, and how farming it would be so much easier than digging around in that rocky old Ozark soil." She snorted. "Wasn't even a year before he decided that was too tedious as well. And besides, there was talk about a strike at Grasshopper Creek, and so off he went. Couldn't talk of anything but Bannack, Oregon, and gold those last few months before he left."

She sensed his stare and froze, spoon suspended in midair, and met his gaze. "My name's Tressie Majors, what's yours?"

He begged for the bite with his soft dark gaze and she gave it, then scraped noisily all around the bowl for every last morsel. He licked some off the corner of his mouth and darted a quick glance toward the pot on the fire.

She held the empty bowl a moment, challenged him, "I said, my name's Tressie Majors, what's yours?"

"Bannon. Reed Bannon. And I thank you, ma'am, for—" He broke off and lifted the thin coverlet. "Who in thunderation stole my clothes?" With that he pulled the quilt tight up under his chin and turned the brightest red Tressie had ever seen a man turn.

She felt a grin coming on and let it happen. There hadn't been a whole lot to laugh at lately, and it felt kind of good.

"Would you like another bowl of mush, Mr. Bannon? There's plenty."

Any attempt to ignore him lying there nearly naked failed. It wasn't easy to pretend this was an ordinary day and there wasn't a dead horse in the yard. And that she hadn't just buried Mama and that newborn babe out there on the prairie. And she wasn't a young defenseless woman all alone with a stranger in this place with no human habitation for fifty miles or more.

Heat flushed her throat and cheeks so she must have looked much like he had a few moments earlier. Fear came and went, left only a sense of relief. At last she had someone to talk to. A man who blushed, and was near starved and who called her ma'am. Her mind echoed the lingering thought that he might be a killer, and she sobered somewhat, but it didn't last. No sense being foolish.

She fetched him another bowl of mush and offering the first bite asked, "Who shot you, Mr. Bannon?"

He raised thick brows, lips tightening and nostrils flaring like he smelled something bad.

But he didn't answer right away, just swallowed slowly.

She waited awhile, sitting there holding up the empty spoon. Then she cut him a hard look so he'd know that this time she meant business.

"I need to know if someone is going to ride up on us in the middle of the night, finish the job they started on you, and then do God knows what to me. I need to know that if you're going to remain under my roof, Reed Bannon."

"And if they are, will you kick me out? Not even let me have the rest of that?" He gestured and she gave him another bite. He swallowed it down and went on, "Maybe mount me on that poor old wore-out horse and send me on my way. You don't appear to be that kind of woman, if you'll excuse my saying so, ma'am."

At the mention of his horse, Tressie looked away. Should she tell him the bony old nag was dead? She gritted her teeth. "Just tell me about that." She pointed the spoon at his bandaged shoulder.

He sighed with a weariness that made her almost ashamed she had asked. "That old horse out there?"

She gulped and nodded. Had he guessed?

"I stole him from a Union soldier in St. Louis and the no-good so and so shot me for my troubles. Hell, they had a whole corral of the beasts and I was afoot with a long way to go."

She gaped at the man. "You just walked up and took a horse that belonged to the United States Army?"

"Union, I said Union. Not United States. Price's blue-bellies massacred us at Prairie Grove, and us that could walk away wasn't feeling too kindly toward those boys, you can bet. I didn't mind a little payback, seeing as how I liked to starved just getting to St. Louis."

"You were a butternut?"

"Butternut hell. I was in McCulloch's army. Me and thousands of others. Indians fought there. We didn't turn our back on our kind, like some did." He aimed the accusation directly at her. Folks from Missouri were not looked too kindly upon by southerners.

She hurried to get away from that aspect of the conversation but continued to feed him. "But you're not wearing a uniform. Are you still in the...in the Rebel Army?"

Reed squirmed. "Look, I'm tired. I'd rather just finish that off and go to sleep, if you don't mind. We can hash this out later, when I'm feeling more up to defending myself against a little mite of a thing who hasn't the slightest idea of what war is all about."

"I know what they call a man who runs away from battle," she snapped. "But you go ahead and sleep now, if you've a mind to. As long as I know some owlhoot isn't going to sneak up on us in the night to get his vengeance against you. I would think that Union soldiers have a little more to do than chase one ratty deserter halfway across the plains."

He reared off the pillow, then grimaced with pain, clutching at the shoulder.

Immediately she regretted the words. She shouldn't have pushed him so far when he was so sorely wounded. The wisest move would be to wait till he got better to finish this argument.

Besides, there were other, more pressing things to worry about. She had no idea what might happen tomorrow or the next day, but for right now things were looking up. Despite the story he told—and she wondered if all the truth had come out—his troubles could be handled in their own time.

What was important was that he looked like he might live. And though they had no transportation and only the tiny amount of money she had hidden away, as soon as Reed Bannon had recovered enough, she would get him to take her to Grasshopper Creek and the gold camps in search of Papa. He had to know what horrible thing he had done. He had to pay somehow for killing Mama and the tiny boy-child.

Two

After the brief recovery, Tressie's visitor lapsed into deep slumber. For a long while she tarried beside the bed, watching the rise and fall of his chest, gazing at the long dark lashes that lay on his gaunt cheeks. She was still enough of a child to let her imagination produce the most fabulous of fantasies about being carried away by a man like this. Oh, granted, he would be better nourished, perhaps more muscular, but with the same glorious golden skin and jet-black hair, the sad dark eyes, the mysterious past of this stranger.

Shaking off such nonsense, she fetched the Kentucky rifle and possible bag and lit out in pursuit of the long-eared jackrabbit of the plains. Food was what this man needed most, now that his wound had been seen to. He must grow strong if he was to take her out of this place, set her in the direction of her runaway coward of a father.

Thoughts like that brought tears to her eyes, even as she stalked her prey.

When she was little, Papa would play with her, toss her high in the air, rub at her tummy with his soft beard and growl until she crowed with delight. And Mama loved him so, her hazel eyes following his movements around the place. Sometimes Tressie would catch her paused at her work, standing stock-still and gazing with adoration at Papa as he went about his own chores. And at night, in the small cabin, she would pretend sleep while they whispered and rustled around on the shuck bed. By then Tressie was a young lady, and so Papa was content to tousle her red hair in passing and call her his sweet daughter. He never ceased to tell her how much she resembled her beautiful mother.

Plodding along, she let her thoughts overpower her need to be alert. The jack bounded from a clump of grass off to her right, catching her unawares. She hastily leveled the gun, drew bead, and fired, missing the dodging critter and chunking up dust in his fleeing shadow.

"Dum, durn," she muttered, and stopped to reload the rifle, chiding herself to pay more attention. The empty cavity in her belly did likewise, and the spirit of the man who could well be her salvation appeared to scold her for having failed.

It was nearly an hour later, and several miles northwest of the cabin, before she scared up another rabbit. This time she didn't miss.

She carried the limp, scrawny beast by the hind legs, his long ears trailing in the grass. Perspiration trickled from under her arms and down the middle of her back and the rifle grew heavy by the time she arrived back home. The horse carcass begged for attention, but first she drew some water, put it on to boil, and cleaned the rabbit. Once the stew was simmering over the fire, she turned her thoughts to the poor dead animal outside. It would be a fearsome job hacking it up in small enough pieces to drag away from the cabin, but it was something that had to be done.

Just thinking about it made her nauseous, but with stoic determination she got out Papa's ax and laid it on the hearth.

Over on the corn-husk bed, Reed Bannon groaned and murmured scarcely intelligible words. She went to him, laid the back of one hand on his forehead. Feverish. Pray God he didn't get infection in the wound and go and die on her despite her care. Then she'd have two critters to haul away. This one would have to be buried as well.

She shook her head with determination. One thing at a time, girl. Papa always said that, didn't he? Fine one to hold up as an example; still, the words rang true. Concentrate. Get the horse taken care of while the stew cooked.

Bannon wet his dry lips and smacked. She went to the bucket and dipped out a cup of cold water. He couldn't seem to drink from the tin rim, so she moistened a clean cloth and touched it to the pitifully cracked mouth. He made a soft sound down in his throat and sucked at the rag; his Adam's apple bobbed as he swallowed and he blindly followed the cloth when she moved it away.

When she brought him more water, the backs of her fingers touched the stubble of his gaunt cheek. Her eyes filled. She didn't even know this man, but she had to save him in order to survive. Watching his helplessness, the need became more than just that. She didn't want him to die, for it would cause her great sorrow. So much death, too much.

The fire crackled and popped and Bannon uttered soft little sounds down in his throat.

Mesmerized by his desperate need, she laboriously fed him water until he fell back into a restless slumber.

During the remainder of that day and far into the night she fed him from the pot of rabbit stew as many times as he would take even a spoonful of the savory liquid. In between she took care of the horrendous task of removing the horse, limb by limb. She hacked off a portion of one shank and added pieces of the meat to the stew pot that also contained a portion of dried vegetables from the root cellar.

In starlit darkness, she finally bathed naked beside the well and went inside to fall into an exhausted slumber on her pallet beside the fire. All night she tended the flames so the stew would continue to cook. It could be another day before the horsemeat was tender enough to eat, but its sweet flavor would add richness to the gamy taste of jackrabbit.

By morning the gray cast had faded from Reed Bannon's skin and the raging fever was down. He looked hearty in a way he hadn't before, and she rejoiced. He would live.

Several days later, the first evening he rose from the sickbed to eat at the table, she hit him with her proposition.

"You want me to what?" he demanded between mouthfuls of horsemeat stew.

The glow of the kerosene lamp threw shadows across the sharp planes of his face, making him look fearsomely savage.

His reaction annoyed and surprised her, considering what she had done for him. But that really wasn't fair, either. He had no idea how close he had come to dying, and certainly had no notion of what her lot had been. It was no use blaming him for the harshness of existence on the prairie.

Undaunted, she repeated her request. "Take me to the gold camps. Help me find my father." "Do you have any notion what you're asking?" Reed drank noisily from the bowl.

"This stuff's almost good. Could I have more?"

"What do you mean, almost? You don't need to go complaining about the fixings." She ladled his bowl full again. She didn't tell him that a chunk of his horse flavored the soup, but instead kept at her demands. "I'm a good shot. I wouldn't be any trouble. You've ate my soup and slept in my bed and took to my waiting on you." Her face grew hot remembering how she'd daydreamed about this man as if he were a knight in shining armor, come to rescue her from her wicked and evil stepmother.

"And I'm grateful."

The terse words put an end to her ramblings. He eyed her over the rim of the bowl he'd lifted to his mouth, black eyes reflecting flashes of orange from the glowing coals of the fire.

He was a devilishly attractive man, she couldn't deny that, but he had a way of provoking her.

She tightened her lips to prevent losing her temper altogether. "But not grateful enough to help me, is that right?"

How dare he deny her this? She had brought him back from death's bidding when she could have let him die. It would have been easier. Yet she was glad she had saved him despite the extra work his being here caused. Not the least had been getting rid of that awful dead horse, chopping its body up with the ax so she could drag the chunks of carcass far away from the cabin before it began to rot and draw vermin. It had been a horrendous job and ended in making her sick.

And what did he say when he found out? Just "Poor damned animal. I should have took better care."

Reed made short work of the horsemeat stew, steadfastly refusing to discuss her request any more. He unfolded his long and lanky frame, dressed now in the spare shirt and pants from his saddlebags. Only a few days of eating at her table and he looked less like a skeleton clothed in loose skin. He glanced at her but said nothing. Unlike most men around a young woman, he seemed not to notice that she was female except for expecting her to cook and clean and fetch for him. So far he hadn't talked about himself or why he had been riding across the plains, wounded and half starved.

Stepping out into the yard, Bannon swung his arms in cautious circles, still favoring the right one. Even before leaving his bed, he had begun to exercise the wounded shoulder, and she enjoyed watching when he wasn't aware of her presence. Taking such pleasure in the sight of a man made her feel just the least bit shameful. What would he think if he knew?

Cleaning the supper dishes in water heated in the empty soup pot took little time, and afterward she, too, went outside. By then he had abandoned his arm swinging. She found him standing straddle-legged beyond the well, gazing west into the purple and gold dusk. A hankering to be gone was written on his boldly etched features. She knew what he wished. And she knew, too, that if she didn't do something, he would light out. He was just itching to be free of her. Wanted to loosen his shackles and head for the setting sun, not once looking back. Like Papa, maybe like most men, for all she knew.

The thought of being alone again, of waking one morning to find this man gone, wracked her body with shudders. Somehow she had to prevent that.

A soft prairie breeze whipped away the last of the sweat from her body, and she lifted her arms to let the air play through the thin dress. She stood that way in silence for a while, then said, "We could walk down to the Platte in two or three days if we kept a good pace."

He didn't answer right away, just sighed and shifted his weight, hanging both thumbs into the waistband of his worn pants. She could feel him weighing her words, considering other possibilities. Finally he spoke. "And then what would we do?"

"Work a spell in Cozad, earn enough money to pay our way into Oregon Territory."

"Why ain't you just done that in the first place?"

She rubbed at the hollow of her throat, unconsciously settling an open hand just above her breasts.

Uncommonly conscious of his studious gaze, she raised her eyes to his. "A woman alone can't go traipsing off to the goldfields. Do you know what would happen to me? I can't take care of myself all by myself, you ought to know that. I'm not big enough nor strong enough, and I'm too particular."

Reed chuckled. "Particular?"

Even when he was making her mad, she admired the way humor enhanced his solemn features. "Oh, yes, mister smarty. I'm particular, and I guess I have that right! I suppose you think that any woman ought to just be grateful for anything a man might send her way. And he could be any kind of man, too, I reckon. With dribbles of tobacco juice running down his chin and stinking worse than your old dead horse. Well, no, thank you, Mr. Bannon."

Before she finished she knew she'd let herself get too worked up for her own good and said more than she intended. Reed was bound to make the most of it. He enjoyed funning and he didn't disappoint her.

"And this man you might be looking for. Just how perfect would he have to be?"

He appeared to be getting a lot of enjoyment from the conversation. She wasn't sure whether to let go her anger and enjoy the moment or pursue her thought.

"I am not looking for me a man," she said. "Suit me just fine if I never had to lay eyes on one again, but the good Lord did see fit to put men and women on this earth for each other, suited and needful as we are. So I guess I just don't have much choice. But I'll tell you this, Reed Bannon." She rounded on him, propping her hands on her hips. "I'm going to Bannack before winter sets in. If you don't take me, then I guess I'll have to find me someone who will. If I stay out here, I'll die, and that's the truth." With that she whirled and marched back toward the cabin so he couldn't see she was about to bust out crying.

Darkness had fallen to the ground, though the sky gleamed like silver around early sparkles of stars. She heard only the roar of a wild fury that blotted out the nasty burring of a rattler in her path. Quicker than lightning, Bannon hit her from one side, knocking her away as the diamondback struck. She landed hard, gasping to regain her breath. At first she had no idea what had happened, but on rising to a crouch saw Reed Bannon where he'd landed on hands and knees, facing down the snake. Without a weapon, no rock or stick in sight, he hunkered there like a granite rock staring head on at the thing. The rattler, already foiled by its first strike at her had coiled once again and renewed the chilling reverberations. She could barely make out the shadowy triangular head, swaying and darting one side to the other, forward then backward.

He didn't move, scarcely breathed as he calmly watched that snake make up its mind whether to let him live or not—and it not two feet from his eyes. Whatever fear held her in its grip turned loose and she scrabbled around on the ground until she came up with a few rocks smaller than her own fist.

"Don't do that," Reed hissed between clenched lips. "Don't rile her."

She eased the intended ammunition to the ground. Whispered, "I'll go get the rifle. Just hold real still. I'll go get the rifle." Because she couldn't bear to turn her back on the terrifying spectacle, she scrabbled backward, using her heels to propel herself.

When man and viper faded into the rapidly falling dusk, she stumbled to her feet and raced for the soddy. A smoldering fire cast towering shadows in the sparse room. Holding the heavy rifle in one hand, she fumbled at a cap with shaking fingers and dropped it. Muttering, she fetched another and managed to fit it over the nipple of the loaded weapon. Thank God for Papa's instructions.

Back outside in the blackening night, she could barely make out Reed and, inches in front of him, still performing a deadly and noisy dance, the coiled rattler. She swiped across her eyes with the fingers of one hand, then snugged the stock of the heavy rifle into her shoulder. Reed took a ragged breath that spooked the snake. The head made a warning pass and he jerked to one side.

Squinting her left eye, she sighted down the long barrel and looked into the indistinct coiled mass of death. It was a long shot, but there was no time left. She squeezed the trigger and clenched her teeth when the hammer ignited the powder with an enormous bang that exploded a ball out the barrel.

The body of the deadly reptile flew apart, bits of meat and hide scattering. In the echoes of thunderous noise Reed's words hung like a prayer. "Blowed her to hell, blowed her plumb straight to hell."

She lowered the butt of the rifle to the ground and spewed out a breath. "And I'll thank you, Reed Bannon, not to call that snake a her one more time."

By then he had tottered back onto his butt. There he rocked, his laughter growing, pealing into the stillness of dusk on the prairie. It was hard, after a while, not to join him simply for the sheer joy of it. Never mind what she'd said wasn't the least bit funny, and that he was probably making light of her once again. Soon her merriment rivaled his.

As quickly as his laughter came, it went, and he lay back, covering his eyes with the crook of an elbow. The right arm with its wounded shoulder lay across his stomach, quivering.

When she could finally get her breath and speak, she said, "We'd best get in the house before that snake's mate comes out to see what all the excitement's about."

He reached up toward her. "I reckon I'm going to need some help getting up. Must still be a might weak."

She took his hand, felt the trembling in his muscles, and hoisted him to his feet. The episode had frightened him more than he cared to let on and he'd covered that fear with laughter.

For support, Reed's other hand spread flat and warm on her back, and she was ashamed that he could tell she wore nothing under the dress. Long ago her undergarments had shredded away. She shrugged out from under his sizzling touch.

"You can walk on your own, Bannon."

He jerked his hand back, as if burned. "Sorry." He lit out for the house, leaving her to tote the rifle.

She'd hurt his feelings and she hadn't intended to. No need to be so sharp with the man. He had, after all, taken her place as a target for the deadly snake. And could well have died for his effort. By the time she got in the door, he had poked a straw from the broom into the fire's coals and relit the kerosene lamp.

She glanced quickly at him, then sat down at the table to clean the rifle

Reed lowered himself in the cane-bottom chair opposite her and watched in silence. Then abruptly both started to say something, halted, started again.

"You go first," he finally said.

"No, you."

"Well, hell, woman. Can't I even be gallant?"

"Gallant?" An odd word to come from his lips.

He studied his blunt fingernails. "I was trying. You saved my life, and I wanted to say thank you, to tell you I appreciated your caring enough. Hell, you could have just come back to the house and waited. Sooner or later, me or that old snake, one would have give in. You might have been rid of me that way."

"I don't want rid of you. Besides, you were only in that spot 'cause you pushed me aside. What I want is to go with you, that's all. And you can see I'd be useful. Your shoulder wouldn't take to firing a rifle, even if you had one, which you don't unless you steal mine. I wouldn't hold you back or anything."

Anger flushed his bronze complexion. "And what makes you think I'd steal your blamed old gun…? Never mind. How old are you, girl?"

"I'll be eighteen soon."

"Holy crow. How soon?"

"A few months."

"How many?"

She jammed the rag deep into the rifle's barrel and tugged it back out before answering. She had a little trouble holding her temper with this man, and she certainly didn't want to tell him that she wouldn't be eighteen until the following February. Have him treat her even more like a child than he already did.

"What difference does it make? I buried my mother after helping her birth a child, and it was dead, too. I reckon I'm full grown after that."

He leveled a hard look at her, the black eyes like chips of flint. Easy to see he didn't want to sympathize with her predicament. When she'd told him, he'd simply turned away to keep from viewing her grief. That had been back when he still lay in the bed too weak to move about. And she'd brought him not only every meal but a vessel to relieve himself in. She'd seen enough that she ought not to cringe at bodily functions, male or female. And she hadn't. But he had been embarrassed by the situation, she could tell, and certainly was in no mood to say he was sorry over her troubles. They were in the past, and survival was here and now.

"It was better, you know," he whispered, and she gave him a quick glance. Moisture glinted in his eyes gone all soft and velvety. "The baby, I mean. Without your mama it would have died anyway, making it all the harder for you, loving it and all."

"I know," she said, and lowered her gaze once more to measuring out the black powder.

What kind of man was this, anyway?

He cleared his throat and stood. "I'm not sleeping in that bed anymore. You take it, and I'll sleep on the floor. My shoulder's all but healed."

She nodded. "You going to take me to town with you?"

"Dammit, girl!"

She bit her lip and rose, hefting the loaded rifle in both hands. After putting it back in its place, she blew out the lamp and went to the bed, where she kicked off her ungainly shoes and lay down fully clothed. She longed to sleep naked once again, yet she dared not with this man on the place.

Back in Missouri Papa and Mama had finally given up on

civilizing their little mountain nymph. Papa would laugh and chide Mama to let her be till she got full grown. That would soon enough see her wearing clothing, he'd bet. The hint that he would take a hand at the proper time warned Tressie and soothed Mama some.

She wondered what this man would think if he knew that about her. It didn't matter, though.

He would go soon and leave her here. She might have survived the wilds of the forest, but this punishing and unforgiving plain that stretched from horizon to horizon would kill her. She hated being able to see so far and behold absolutely nothing. What a lonesome feeling.

While Reed bedded down noisily on the floor, she turned her back so he wouldn't hear her crying. With all her heart she wanted to curl up in Mama's rocker and pretend that wonderful soul's arms were wrapped around her, soothing away the hurt and fear.

Reed shifted on the floor and grunted in surprised pain. She held her breath. He was awake, she could tell by the noises he made. She had never been more conscious of his presence in the cramped room.

The muscles of her stomach tightened when he cleared his throat and spoke. "I never knew women, so maybe sometimes I'm too harsh."

She didn't reply, just took a noisy breath to clear her clogged nostrils.

"Aw, hell. You ain't crying, are you?"

She still refused to answer.

His lazy voice came to her out of the dark. "My mother, she died birthing me. They said I come right out into my daddy's arms, him a cursing every screaming breath I took for paining his woman so. He come in there to kill me, they said, but my grandmother wouldn't let him. Mama was a Dakota Sioux. Bright Fox by name. Pa was a trapper, and when she died he just rode away and left me with them. Never came back."

She waited for him to continue, and when he didn't, asked, "And you were raised by Indians?"

"For a spell. Hell, I may look more white than red, but I'm still a breed. I finally run off soon after I became a man. I was twelve." He shifted again and groaned softly.

"Reed?"

"Huh?"

"If your shoulder is paining you, you could sleep in the bed."

"No, you stay there. I'm okay."

"I didn't intend to leave…just move over."

"Oh." The word huffed out of his mouth to overpower the silence. "Well, I don't know."

"I'm dressed and so are you. No sense in you hurting." Her heart pounded in her throat until she couldn't speak. What did it mean that she was willing to use her body to get her way with this man? Did that make her a soiled woman or just a survivor? The sounds of him rising from the floor quickened her pulse. With shaking fingers, she unbuttoned the front of her dress as he lowered his body to the edge of the shuck mattress.

He lifted one leg, then the other before lying back. She turned toward him and lay the flat of her palm on the taut muscles of his stomach. Reed sucked in a quick breath. After a while he put his hand over hers and she guided it to one bare breast.

The calloused fingers lay still. She gazed into the reflections of firelight his eyes sent into hers. Those beautiful black eyes that revealed so much of his vulnerability. What strengths he might have possessed had been sapped away by his injury, but she sensed them like an underlying current felt but not seen. As he grew stronger would this man desert her, too?

She leaned forward and he moved his palm firmly over her breast. She shivered. Despite her well-laid plans to entrap this man, his first tender touch awoke a slumbering passion within her soul. Hard work and deprivation had disguised the woman growing inside her, and to deal with her awakening presented her with a problem. She was about to enjoy what had started out to be a ploy to trick this man.

He licked his lips and tilted his head, studying her face closely in the firelight. With a quizzical look that defied understanding, he cupped her ear with one palm and raised to take her full lips to his.

She forgot her mission and rested in the warmth of his bare chest, a great joyful sigh bursting from her. She twisted both hands into his long hair and held on, not knowing what to do next, their lips together softly.

After the kiss he held her in silence, his breath a mist against her cheek. Oddly confused, speaking now of his earlier puzzlement, he said, "Tressie? I feel like we've been together before, but I can't…Did we…?"

"Just a dream. Maybe we're fated."

A favorite term of Grammy's. Folks were often fated for one thing or another, and Tressie could accept that. If she could convince Reed Bannon, maybe he could accept it, too. He held her close, her head tucked against his shoulder. Was something wrong with him, that he made no further move?

He shivered and his warm skin rippled where her small hand lay. "Whatever we do, it's just from our needs," he said down in his throat. "That's all, you understand? It don't mean anything, Tressie."

It was about to happen. Her first time. Surely she couldn't let this stranger be the one who would steal her virginity forever. She closed her eyes, said a little prayer begging forgiveness.

"Oh, yes, yes, it does mean something," she whispered. It meant trapping him, putting him in a position that would keep him from leaving her alone and going on his way. She could make him want her so badly he'd have to take her with him. At the same moment, an overpowering need to have him close as only a lover can be grew deep in her soul.

She leaned forward, traced with her tongue the laddering of his ribs, then delicately kissed the firm slant of his whiskered jaw. "Take me with you, please."

He spanned her tiny waist with both hands and murmured her name then turned his head so that their mouths met again.

A moan flowed from his throat to hers. His need, his almost helpless desire rose to surround her. Lost in her own passion, she almost forgot why she had started this deception. She was supposed to be seducing him into taking her out of here. Promising him more joys to come if only he'd let her go with him.

With each groan of his rapture, she rejoiced. She would make him want her so desperately that he couldn't possibly give her up. Yet she couldn't stop the heated thrum of her own passion.

He embraced her, held her close, his breath coming in great gasps. She had worked the magic, and in the process been caught up in it herself, desiring nothing but for this moment to last forever. What a strange and wonderful feeling this was, this wanting of another human being.

She marveled at it, but she had to control herself. Had to be in charge, had to hold back. This was neither the time nor the place to yield her virginity. And certainly not to a man who wandered around the country, probably no better than Papa when it came to commitment.

"This isn't right. You're just a child." He pushed her away with what meager strength he had.

At the same moment she did the same, glad of his frailty, annoyed at his reference. But that was of little consequence. She didn't want to actually do it, not in Mama and Papa's bed. She needed him to know what he could have if he took her with him, that was all. Thank goodness he didn't insist.

Unexpectedly he grabbed her wrist, his strength surprising.

For a brief moment her heart hammered in her throat. Was he going to force it after all? Maybe she couldn't overpower him in the throes of passion. Suppose he decided to force her?

"You should not tempt a man like that, child. It could backfire on you." His voice was harsh, angry.

She moved quickly away, turned so that she lay facing the wall until her breathing evened out and the strange throbbing between her legs passed.

So this was what it felt like to want a man. She wondered at the overpowering surge of desire that had exploded in the pit of her stomach, gripped her so that her breasts ached and a living warmth flowed through her being. What a joyous feeling.

Beside her, Bannon moved and she stiffened. If he touched her again, she wouldn't be able to resist. But he sighed and settled once more. She wanted to ask him right out without preamble if he was going to take her with him when he left. After all, he only thought her a child indulging in a game, seeing as how she had cheated him of his reward.

A tear leaked from the corner of one eye and she rubbed it away angrily. Why were men the ones who made all the decisions, when life affected the woman so harshly?

Three

The *squee-squee* of prairie hens announced the coming of morning and awoke Tressie before daylight. To her distress the other side of the bed was empty. He'd gone and left her. She scrambled from the bed and stood in the open doorway, staring toward the horizon. A figure moved through the distant silver glow of dawn. It could be no one but her bed partner of the previous night escaping as fast as he could.

"Damn you, Reed Bannon. Damn you to hell." The wind tossed the shouted words back in her face.

Hugging herself, she thought of the night before and shivered. How could he make her feel the way he had and then just walk away as if it were nothing? The louse. He wasn't going to get away with this.

Back inside, his saddlebags were gone, stuffed no doubt with his few belongings of which she knew nothing. She dug through her own meager supply of clothing and came up with overalls and an old shirt of Papa's. Shrugging into them, she fashioned a poke from another shirt. She filled it with such supplies as she could find: half a bag of cornmeal, some salt, the last few vegetables from the root cellar. If Bannon had waited, they could have packed up a proper supply for the trip. How could he have run away without so much as a fare-thee-well?

And after she had saved his life, too.

She tied the poke, slipped it over the barrel of the Kentucky rifle, and strapped the possible bag around her waist. Black powder, balls, and caps were almost as necessary as food if they were to survive the long trek across the vast Dakota territory. At the door she stuck bare feet into the only pair of shoes she owned and laced them tightly because they were too big. As an afterthought she grabbed an old felt hat from its hook on the wall and plopped it onto her head. It would keep off the punishing rays of the sun.

She was almost out the door before she remembered Mama's few hoarded coins tied in a hanky and stuffed down in the bedding. Rustling around in the dry corn shucks, she retrieved the handful of silver and crammed the pouch in the front pocket of her overalls. Her gaze was caught by Mama's rocker and a sob tore from deep in her throat.

Fear of the unknown combined with the sudden attack of forlorn sorrow threatened to keep her there, in the company of what she knew. But then memories of the previous winter intruded. The bitter cold of the stark and endless days and nights; and later the scratching and hoeing in the dirt to raise what scraggly vegetables would grow in this hellhole. And always the loneliness. Memories of that and the loss of her family chased her from the soddy without a backward glance.

She turned away from thoughts of the life she had once had, and toward the man making tracks across the prairie. If she ran at a decent pace she could catch him when he bedded down for the night. The infernal wind pelted her with grit and powdery dust, but she ran on, ignoring its sting. Past the well and then the graves, not giving either a sideways glance. Going and not coming back. What she left she would just have to leave.

For a while she tried to keep the shrinking figure in sight while she trotted, but too many times she stumbled over

clumps of grass or into prairie dog holes. Finally she decided
to follow by tracing his passing through the brittle tufts of
grama grass. He had veered to the north, scuffing along and
leaving a trail that, while not easy to follow, was temporarily
visible. No doubt of where he was going. Headed a little north
of west, just like all the others in their quest for gold.

Before Papa lit out for Grasshopper Creek, he had
traced the way in the dirt of the soddy floor. Her knowledge
of geography was limited to the Ozarks and their long trek
north into Dakota Territory. She had been to Cozad, where
they bought supplies, and it lay fifty miles or more to the
south down on the Platte River and the well-traveled Oregon
Trail. Reed Bannon was going toward the gold strikes with no
notion of either Cozad or the Oregon Trail.

A grumbling stomach and the climbing sun announced
dinner time. Stopping only long enough to tear off a chunk of
withering cabbage, she stuffed it in her mouth and marched on.
She gnawed at the tough leaves, welcoming the bit of moisture
they offered. How stupid of her to have walked right past the
well without realizing she needed water for the journey. She
could only hope that Bannon had better sense. The inside of her
mouth turned to dust as the heat of the June day bore down.
She would surely choke.

When she first heard the deep, earthshaking rumbling,
she thought it was a buffalo stampede. She'd heard men talk of
such, but had never seen for herself the sight of countless shaggy
beasts on the rampage, carpeting the land from sky to sky in
all directions. Kicking up dust so thick it blotted out the sun.
They stopped for nothing. But then out here, there wasn't much
to stop for. Except this morning there was Reed Bannon and
Tressie Majors. Both easy targets. Their trampled bodies would
scarcely cause a thud under the hooves of such animals.

As the sun slid farther west and still no buffalo, she

spotted thunderheads boiling up ahead. Masses of black clouds swallowed up the tin-metal sky. The hot wind whipped around, shifted abruptly. She shoved the hat to the back of her head and studied the progress of the storm for a few precious moments. Her nostrils quivered, picked up the tart smell of rain. As quickly as that she shifted her attention back in the direction Bannon had taken, and saw only vast emptiness. He was gone! How could she have lost sight of him so fast? By running and not stopping for anything, she should have shortened the distance between them in the hours since her departure. Whirling, she looked back the way she had come. No sign of the soddy anymore. Panicked, she turned a complete circle, confused and frightened. The vast emptiness terrified her. She could wander around and around for days and not know it.

That, of course, was ridiculous. All she had to do was use the sun to get her bearings. It traveled almost precisely east to west, having only this week passed the summer solstice. Still, the darkening clouds would soon blot out its guiding rays. She needed to find a landmark to head for before she no longer had anything to go by. Once rain fell, his scant trail would be washed away. There was nothing on the hateful, treeless plains but grass. Making up her mind, she pointed her nose a little north of the sun where it disappeared into the massive black clouds, and began to trot. After a while she settled into a faster pace, and only slowed occasionally to shift the heavy rifle from one arm to the other.

The overheated land turned somber and threatening and took on a sickly yellow hue. Rumbles of thunder shook the ground, distant fingers of lightning split the sky, and soon sporadic hailstones as big as marbles pelted down. They struck painfully at her shoulders, thunked solidly onto the crown of the hat. On she ran until the ice turned to rain and the thirsty soil drank its fill before turning to mud. The aroma of wet grasses and sweet earth raced with the scampering wind, north toward the Black Hills and back again. She swept off the hat and threw back her head to catch the welcome moisture in her mouth. All too soon she was gasping within the cold, wet embrace of icy rain.

Thunder and lightning pushed the storm ever southeast, the deadly charges erupting to split apart the glowering sky. Panting, she dropped to her knees. She couldn't go on until this passed. She remembered seeing cows and horses killed by such vicious bolts of fire. Back in the Ozarks she often watched in awe as balls of flame zigzagged through the trees. Carrying the gun in the open was inviting sudden death.

Placing the filthy hat beside her so it would catch the rain, she chose to lay low until the storm passed. Hugging the poke to keep it dry, she sprawled out in the clumps of grass. Tiny rivers flowed around her, and minuscule creatures came to life, there had been none.

Where did they come from? Perhaps rained from heaven itself, for surely they hadn't lain buried beneath the ground all these dry months.

At last the brunt of the storm passed over, its noisy departure fading to a low growl and crackle. Soaked through, front-side covered with mud, she rose to take a look around. To the west, feeble fingers of sunlight broke through the scurrying clouds. It made her feel odd to know that the galloping storm was probably drenching the deserted soddy at this very moment, soaking the soil she'd piled on the double grave. She rubbed at her eyes, muddying them with both fists. The knot in her aching throat broke loose in wrenching sobs. The burying had been hard enough, but now to think of them lying beneath the soil down there in the dark while rainwater leaked through the crevices, ran over Mama's beloved face, the baby cradled in both arms, its tiny precious mouth that never uttered a sound. She could scarcely bear thinking about it, and she folded herself into a ball, sobbing without control.

Sucking at the moist air, she swallowed back the sorrow. She mustn't give in. "Don't be such a baby. Just get up and be on your way."

Staggering to her feet, she gulped down the foul tasting water caught in the bedraggled old hat. With a grimace she shoved it onto her head and moved once more into a steady gait across the barren plains. After a while she noticed the muscles in her legs were tightening up and the going seemed harder. How curious. She slowed to get her bearings. Behind her the land fell away so gradually she hadn't noticed it, and ahead lay a gentle upward slope. That was the way of the high plains. Always fooling you, getting the best of you without any warning. She panted her way to the top of the rise and gasped in astonishment. At her feet stretched a luminous green valley through which a river meandered. Dotting its banks were trees that from this distance resembled folks gathered for a baptizing. And just disappearing into that growth moved a figure. It had to be Bannon.

She raised an arm, waved and shouted his name. Of course he couldn't hear her, but much like a child at play, she continued to cry out until her voice grew hoarse. He passed out of sight into the trees. Probably going right on across the river that could only be the North Loup. She pushed back thoughts of crossing the rain-swollen waters alone. Had often heard talk of the North Loup. Rich folks, big business people, had all homesteaded the land along its banks before the Majors came to the territory. Some took as much as four and five sections and then paid poor folks to throw up a shanty and work land they would never own.

What a sight that river valley was! Lush islands of succulent growth along the banks of a sparkling silver ribbon that stretched for miles and miles.

Going downhill toward its banks was much easier as long as she kept her feet under her. The rifle rode hard on her shoulder, the bag banged at her hip, but on she ran knowing only that she had to catch up with him before dark. The sun would soon set. Surely he would stop for the night near water. The land leveled out and she slowed to a walk. In the river bottoms the trees and clumps of shrubbery grew in such thick masses she might walk within yards of him and not know it. She lost sight of the far bank of the river and the valley beyond once she reached flat land. Not very good at judging distances, she could still be as far as two miles behind him. A long way with night approaching, and if he crossed the river and went on, then what? She couldn't much more than dog-paddle, and she certainly couldn't swim strongly enough to overcome a swift current.

The sun rested on the rim of the earth when she finally made the riverbank. Hunkering on her heels, she gazed into rushing swirls of muddy water, made angry by the storm. The current ran mighty fast, the froth and roar enough in itself to frighten her out of crossing, never mind that she couldn't tell how deep the murky water was. Crouched there in the dense shadows of early dusk, she probably was invisible to man and beast. Beneath the thick canopy of cottonwood branches would be an ideal place to spend the night, lulled to sleep by the singing leaves. The forest along the riverbank reminded her a bit of the Ozark wilderness, and she'd spent many a night alone there cradled in the arms of the deep woods. But if he walked on into the night, she would never catch him. Exhausted and confused, she bent to drink, unsure of what to do.

Above the roar of the rushing waters and the wind through the cottonwood trees came the sound of galloping horses. Harsh shouts cut through the rain-washed air. Peering between thick underbrush, she made out several riders upstream and on the far bank of the river. Indians!

Afraid to move, she clapped a hand tightly over her mouth. Fear dried her tongue so that it stuck to her teeth. Obviously the Indian party hadn't seen Bannon, wherever he might be, for several dismounted and let their horses drink while they stretched and spoke casually. A couple even relieved themselves right out in the open. Spying on them sent a chill trailing up and down her backbone. She shuddered. Any moment they might spot her, and that would mean death or worse.

A hailing shout from the bank directly opposite her hiding place fueled her fear. Were there more of the savages? While the Indians were distracted, she edged deeper into the brush. There she huddled as the men grew quite boisterous. She dared a cautious peek. Someone had joined them. A white man. She expected at any moment to see them fall upon him and scalp his hair right off his head. That didn't happen. A friendly visit ensued that seemed endless. Finally the Indians mounted up and rode off, everyone waving friendly-like. She squinted her eyes and glared at the man they left behind. It was...no, it couldn't be. But it was. The man who had spoken so casually with the Indians was Reed Bannon.

An explosive breath from deep in her lungs sounded awfully loud and she hunkered back in hiding, terrified that the Indians would swing around and ride her way. She stayed there until her legs were tingly stumps and a cramp held her back stiff. She'd dropped the rifle in her earlier haste, and so backed out of the brush at long last, bent on retrieving it. She bumped solidly into a pair of legs clothed in soaked britches.

Screeching, she tried to scamper back into hiding. A hand snatched her overall straps and dragged her to her feet. "You can come out now," a stern voice said.

Letting out a yowl, she flailed the air with clenched fists.

Her Kentucky rifle in one hand, the crossed straps of her overalls fisted in the other, Reed Bannon spoke in a soft voice, "Hush, girl. You want to bring them back? Hush, now. Thunderation, what are you doing here?"

"Reed? Is that you?" Blind panic dissolving, she peered into the familiar face. 'Turn me loose this instant. Let me go! And give me back my gun."

She kicked at his shins with the heavy shoes. He dodged easily out of range, grimaced, and let go of her. The shoulder wound had to still be bothering him, but she didn't care. She just landed on both feet with a grunt and glared at him, ready to do further battle.

"Behave yourself. Is that any way to treat the man who just saved your hide?"

"Oh, sure. After leaving me out on the prairie to die, you save my life. How gallant." She took great pleasure in throwing his words back at him.

He ignored it and continued to scold her. "For goodness' sake, I didn't leave you to die. You were safe there. You had a roof over your head, food to eat, water to drink. What do you have out here, girl? Indians and wild animals, that's what. Do you know how many men die crossing these plains? Not to mention the weaker sex. Now what am I going to do with you? Two days lost if I take you home. There ain't many women in the camps. Lord sakes, girl, how can I protect you?"

She seriously considered leaping on him and giving him a good pounding. His eyes snapped and she changed her mind, speaking instead. "Forget that; I'll protect myself. You're not taking me back. Not unless you hog-tie me and drag me. If you do I'll just follow you again."

He snorted in derision. "Hog-tying you isn't such a bad idea." Though she could scarcely see his face in the darkness, she sensed him studying her. "What were you going to do come dark? Or suppose I'd a gone on when I spotted you coming down off that rise, instead of hanging around? Them Indians would have had you if I hadn't sent them off in another direction, and then what would you have done?"

"A lot you care. Taking advantage of me like some animal in heat, then running off. I thought we were— I felt like—"

"Bull hockey, girl. You lured me into your bed trying to weasel your way into my good graces. You think I'd want it so bad I'd take you along so I'd have it at hand? Sorry to disappoint you." His voice held a mocking tone she didn't like.

She doubled up her fist and belted him dead on the point of his chin. The blow jarred her to the top of her head. She sucked at her knuckles and did a dance while he staggered backward.

The jolt didn't knock him off his feet, but his eyes glazed momentarily. "Woman, what's the matter with you?" At least that changed his tone to amazed.

Sucking at her aching fist, she looked up into his black eyes. Eyes that revealed more hurt than anger. She felt the tears coming and could do nothing but let them flow. Down both cheeks they poured and plopped onto the ground. Soon she began to bawl in earnest and slumped to a sitting position. With moisture-laden words she tried to explain her actions, but couldn't make herself understood. Weariness had defeated her.

"Aw, dammit to hell," he said, and knelt beside her. "I ain't never been able to abide a woman crying."

"Well, doe den. Dust doe."

He put an arm around her, swiveled to sit at her side, and hugged her. "Hush up trying to talk, it sounds plumb silly. I reckon you need to cry, just go right ahead and do it. But I want you to get it out of your system, you hear? You can't trail me across this danged prairie bawling like a baby. It just won't do at all."

She nodded and wiped at her nose. Did that mean he was taking her, or was he just having one of his jokes again?

"Here, hell, use this," he said, whipping off his disreputable bandanna. "Don't worry if you get it dirty; we can wash it in the river," he announced solemnly.

She eyed the sweat-stiffened, dust-coated, tattered thing

and giggled. "Hard to get it any dirtier." Before long she was laughing as hard as she'd been crying earlier.

Grumbling, trying to keep a straight face, he snatched the bandanna from her outstretched hand, took it to the riverbank, and sloshed it around awhile. Then he wrung out the piece of worn and faded cloth and brought it back to her. Between laughing and wiping, she got herself cleaned up and settled down, then handed it back.

"Better wash it," she said. That set them both off.

The merriment didn't last long. He sobered first, gesturing upriver. "That was an advance hunting party of Sioux yonder. They're looking for a herd of buffalo, scouting ahead of the rest of the tribe. They'll be here soon and we'll need to be gone."

"Be gone tonight?"

"No, tomorrow'll do."

She could no longer make out his face in the gathering darkness, and she didn't enjoy talking to someone she couldn't see. "Could we build a fire now and eat? I'm hungry."

"No. No fire tonight. We'll sleep here till dawn, then we need to get gone. We should cross the river, then camp, but all things considered, we'd best wait."

She could hardly contain her joy. He was taking her with him. For a while she was content to sit on the ground and embrace that bliss. The feeling didn't last long, for she began to detect the most foul odor. She sniffed at the air. "What is that?"

Reed flared his nostrils. "I don't smell anything."

She shifted and realized the stink came from the two of them. "Oh, I can't stand this," she said, and unfastened the overall galouses. "I'm going to take a bath."

"A what? You're going to do what?"

'Take a bath. It's us I'm smelling, and we stink." She leaned toward him, sniffed. "Yep, you can take a bath, too.

He frowned and made a snorting noise in his throat. "I

knew I'd regret this before we even got started. Just where are we going to take this bath, Miss Priss?"

"In the river, where else?"

"In the dark and all alone?"

"Not all alone. You're going to take one, too. I can't swim, so you'll have to hang on to me so I don't drown."

He sighed loudly. "I just might hold on to you, all right...till you do drown. How would that be? I ain't going in that danged river in the dark. If I was going to do that, we'd just ford her and be on our way this very minute. Now hush up this nonsense and get some sleep. We'll leave at first light."

She climbed to her feet. "I'm taking me a bath before I lay down to sleep."

He made some settling noises as if pawing out a bed, then came his hushed whisper, so soft she could only just make out the words. "With the cottonmouth snakes?"

She thought about that for a beat or two. "You're lying." Such a weak denial.

"Nope. Comes up a rain like this, washes 'em out of their nests around the banks. Sometimes as many as a hundred will be writhing and hissing in one spot. But you do what you want. I'll wait here to drag you out and bury you when they get finished. Frail little thing like yourself, probably a couple a dozen of the varmints latching on to your hide is all it'll take to do you in."

She considered what he said, not sure if he was lying or telling the truth, but not willing to go in the water alone. "Maybe I could just wet that rag of yours and wash a bit."

A long, drawn-out snore was his reply. After listening but not believing the sound of his sleeping, she was attacked by a vision of hordes of snakes, crawling up the bank and slithering across the ground to attack her helpless body. Feeling with her feet, she located Reed's curled form and nested down, spooned against his lanky backside. He went right on with his snoring, like he didn't even know she was there.

Tomorrow they would cross the river and head for Bannack. What awaited them there she couldn't guess, having never learned much about gold rushes and the like. But it would surely beat life alone in a prairie soddy. Wouldn't it?

Four

While Reed shouted instructions over the roar of the river, he lashed their supplies to a raft of cottonwood limbs strapped together with strips of vine. "All you have to do is hang on, keep your head above water, and kick your feet. I'll do the rest."

Setting his lips tightly, he refused to so much as glance in her direction. "I got my doubts we'll make it across the river. Could maybe do it alone, but with this jackleg floating contraption and a woman half scared to death, who can't even swim, I ain't so sure."

He was going to leave her after all. "I can hang on to something. I won't be any trouble."

Head cocked, he looked her up and down as if deciding whether he would bother with her or not. With a sigh, he said, "Tell you one thing girl. If I have to abandon the supplies to rescue you, I don't know if I can. May just let your little head go bobbing away in the current."

He resented having her along; she was holding him up and he wanted to abandon her. If she faltered, that's exactly what he would do, too. Just go right on swimming, dragging along the supplies and leaving her to drown. After all, why should he care? He might even be glad to be rid of her. Even though she didn't really believe he was quite that coldhearted, she was determined to keep up, no matter what it took.

If only she'd learned how to swim. Who could know one day she would be faced with a life-or-death situation on the banks of the ravenous North Loup River? Paddling around in a clear woodland stream or pool was far removed from kicking off into that storm-swollen rush of water that slapped hungrily at her legs, taking a taste of what it would ultimately consume.

His dark eyes regarded her a bit longer, then his lips curled in a smile. He was teasing, like he did once in a while. "Grab a good hold and don't let go." He turned to face their adversary and slipped out of his shirt.

She gulped past a lump in her throat and fixed her gaze on his back. The blades of his broad shoulders stood up like flat paddles. The exit wound high on his right arm shone purple against the coppery skin. Suppose he wasn't strong enough? Would he truly let her go to save himself and the precious supplies? She wanted to ask but thought better of it.

He turned abruptly toward her, catching her gaze with those incredibly dark eyes. A wan smile rippled over the morose features. Without a word he waded into the angry current until it washed at the line wrapped around his chest and under his arms. The raft wobbled and began to move, tightening the lashings.

He shouted back at her, the words nearly lost in the noise of the river. "Don't worry, we can do it. Keep your mouth shut, hang on, kick your feet and hold your breath if you go under."

"Go under?" Already rapidly being dragged into deep water, she set her heels and pulled backward.

"No, you don't," he yelled, and dove in, swimming with surprisingly powerful overhand strokes, towing both the small raft and her right into the swift current.

Terrified, she clung to the ridged pole. "But why can't I float on the logs with our stuff?" The question had no more than tumbled from her trembling lips than the bottom dropped out from under her. Forgetting his instructions, she opened her mouth to scream, got a mouthful of water, and went under. Clutching at the raft, she surfaced, choking and sputtering. Her mind turned black with panic. Where was he? What had he told her to do? She couldn't think.

Surely he wouldn't let her drown, would he? They couldn't survive without their supplies, but he'd do just fine without her.

She coughed out a mouthful of water and squinted her eyes. Up ahead he was barely visible, swimming along. He appeared more desperate dragging at all that dead weight and getting absolutely nowhere. They were being washed downstream, helplessly tossed about like deadwood. Gasping and frantically struggling to keep her head above water, fingers gripping so tight they hurt, she kicked out tentatively and felt just the slightest forward movement. She kicked harder. Her effort was actually helping. Swimming wasn't, after all, so much different than marching across the prairie. Slow and steady for walking, harder and more intense for a fast trot. She concentrated, paddled her feet vigorously, and felt a rush of jubilation as they began to move slowly forward. She was doing it.

Though the pitiful little raft and its crew continued to float east with the current, the opposite bank appeared to inch closer. It was rough going and the river gave grudgingly, until finally her legs and arms grew heavy as stones. If they didn't make it soon, she would have to let go so he could reach shore safely. Despite a valiant effort, her strength began to desert her as the icy cold took its toll. At the very instant when her hands began to slip from the wet raft, both knees struck bottom. The grating blow scraped away skin even through the soaked pants legs, but she scarcely felt the pain. They had made it. Tears filled her eyes. They weren't going to die. She shouted, laughed, gulped in another mouthful of cold water, and choked.

Though in shallower water, he kept crawling along the bottom, head down, heaving like a horse tied to a heavy load. The raft, still caught by the swift current, threatened to pull him back into the river and he shouted, "Help me, Tressie, hang on, push."

She raised her drenched face and with what little energy she had left, shoved the raft onto shore beside him and rolled onto her back. "It's okay, we did it, we made it," she shouted into the clear blue sky.

Still on his hands and knees, he coughed and rocked back and forth. Somehow he couldn't make himself stop.

She crept to his side, laid a hand on the tense muscles rippling across his back. "We made it. We're on the other side."

Tugging on the binding, she dragged the raft even farther up on the bank, out of reach of the hungry river. With a last feeble effort, she collapsed beside him. "We did it. We did it. I thought I'd drown, but we did it. I think I could swim now. Did you see me? I just started paddling my legs, kicking for all I was worth, and—"

"Tressie?"

"What, Reed? What is it?"

"Shut up."

Rolling over onto her back, she gazed up into the inverted bowl of cloudless metallic sky and laughed. She laughed like the child she was, like the child she'd once been, and soon he joined her. They hugged each other, then tried to pick the wet knots loose that held him to the raft.

"Just slip it over your head," she told him while he went on doggedly working at the knotted vine.

Vexed because he continued to ignore her instructions, she knelt in front of him and wrapped cold fingers around his. "Stop, Reed. Just lift up your arms."

He stared at her a moment. She knelt there, all wet and shivery, and grinning like a little kid. Irresistible and very alive. With a soul-deep shudder, he did as she said. They had, after all, both survived. A great cause for celebration. And she had done her share. After she removed the knotted harness, her breasts brushing his goose-pimply flesh, he locked his arms around her in a bear hug. Gazing down into her adorable face, its features still a little tense, full lips trembling from the cold, he had the most insane desire to kiss her. Not the lustful kind of desire she had exposed in him when she'd tricked him into her bed and her arms. But the kind a man feels when he first spots the woman he might want with him always. Still he ought to pull back, for this one was no woman, but merely a child. He couldn't forget that again.

She gazed up into the smoky eyes. For a moment she thought he was going to kiss her. She wouldn't mind at all, but at the last minute he didn't. They knelt there a moment longer, then lay back side by side to let the heat of the sun dry their wet clothing.

Later, feeling rested and jubilant, she rolled to her stomach and propped her chin in both hands to stare at her companion. "Reed?"

He took a deep breath before answering. "What now?"

"How many rivers will we have to cross?"

"That's a question I can't answer. Never toted them up. I know one thing, though; I sure hope you can learn to swim before too many more."

"Well, I was swimming. Along there at the last."

He chuckled and rose to unlash the rifle and their belongings from the crude raft. 'Time we got moving," he said, peering at her through a thick fringe of lashes. "Drink your fill before we leave. I wish we had some way to carry water, but 1 guess we'll just have to hope the storm filled some sump holes along the way. "He hefted the rifle. "You want to carry this?"

Sometime that afternoon they shared a handful of shriveled raw vegetables, chewing as they walked.

"My feet are on fire," she complained later.

'Yeah, but we'll get used to it. They'll blister at first, but after a while they'll harden up. Socks help. You got socks?"

She laughed bitterly. "Where would I get socks?"

He grunted.

Late in the day they came across a sinkhole of spring water surrounded by a few brave shrubs and saplings. After drinking, both slipped out of their shoes and soaked their aching feet.

"How do you know where we're going?" Tressie asked.

"We'll hit the Niobrara sometime tomorrow and then follow it west into Wyoming Territory."

That really wasn't what she had asked, but she nodded, afraid to think about crossing any more rivers. "How come we aren't taking the Platte River Road?"

"No need to go south and then come back north." He lifted his feet out of the water. 'Time we got moving. We can make some more miles before dark."

As it turned out, they didn't make many more miles that day. Their blazing feet gave out at a watering hole some few miles west of their previous stop. Her feet were bleeding inside her shoes, and she had continued to fall farther and farther behind.

Finally she stumbled to both knees and cried out, "Please, can't we stop? I can't even walk."

He turned and limped back to her. Kneeling, he took her arm. "There's water ahead. You have to go just a bit farther. Come on, girl, you can do it."

Rocking in agony, she cried, "How do you know that? Can't we just stop right here?"

He looked around, scanning their exposure. "No. We're too out in the open. Bait is all we'd be."

"Bait for what?" she wailed. "I never saw such godforsaken land. Who in his right mind would be out here?"

"Bears. Indians. White scum. You name it. Come on, up you go." He hoisted her to her feet. She jerked her arm away. He was probably only trying to scare her, and it was working.

"Okay. I can walk myself."

He grinned a bit, admiring her spunk. She could still argue

with him, but he wasn't sure how much longer she would last. Anything could be out here, including things they couldn't see. He'd watched invisible sicknesses wipe out whole parties in a scant few weeks. Indians and wild animals weren't all they had to worry about. Barring everything else, they could simply starve to death.

He lifted his head and sniffed at the sweet smell of water carried in the wind. She tottered along behind, each step a torture that drove spikes of blackness through her vision, blotting out the sun. But she couldn't, she wouldn't give up. Not even if her feet turned to stumps. She put her mind on other things. Wondering about Reed Bannon. How could he just find water the way he did? Must be something to do with his Indian upbringing. All she wanted to know was how far it was to Grasshopper Creek.

By the time they reached the sand hills she had lost track of the days. And gazing out across the wavering sands, she wondered why she had bothered to survive the trek only to end up on the brink of hell itself. After the initial shock, she shaded her eyes with the brim of her hat and squinted into the distance.

"I didn't know there was a desert out here."

"I guess there's just about everything you could imagine in this part of the country, with the exception maybe of oceans." Crossing his legs, Reed sank to his butt in the cool sand.

They had been under way since before dawn, and the rising sun hadn't yet warmed the earth, having just cleared the horizon at their backs. It would soon turn this world into a flaming hell.

He propped the rifle over one shoulder and studied the terrain in a way that had become familiar to her. Legs spread apart, he would gaze off into the distance with every appearance of sleeping. It was an unmoving stance that usually accompanied total silence.

On the other hand, she could only be so patient, and after a while she wandered away to explore their new surroundings.

With a great scurrying and flurrying of sand, something leaped from behind a growth of scrub. She yelped. A tiny rodent that had landed a few paces away regarded her with beady eyes, nose whiskers twitching. The animal resembled a mouse, but with a tuft on its long stringy tail. She got that much of a look at the strange creature before it bounded high into the air, kicking sand every which way. Giggling with delight, she followed the animal's springy progress. Obviously totally unafraid, he would pause occasionally, seat himself on rather long hind legs, and tuck miniature front feet neatly under his chin. She would have sworn he was saying, "Well, come on, let's go."

What a delightful pet he would make. Each time she approached tentatively, ready to make friends, the mouse would zip away in a blur of flying sand, causing her to yelp once again.

Those squeals finally disturbed Reed's reverie and he went in search of her. His mind still on the best way of crossing the sand hills, he finally caught up with her, playing tag with a damned mouse. And having quite a time of it, too, he reckoned. How wonderful to be able to find enjoyment in such a simple game.

He watched her squat down beside a clump of grass to giggle in delight at the mouse's antics. Her hair, shagging over the collar of the rough shirt, flamed in splashes of early morning sun. Sometime in the past few days she had ripped off the legs of the overalls above her knees. While he admired the view, her willingness to expose so much of her body perplexed him. He'd never known a woman to do that.

Well, at least not a woman like her.

Really more a kid than a grown female.

He chuckled at his silent attempts to explain his own judgments to himself, and she turned at the sound.

"Did you see that?" she shouted, clapping her hands. "A mouse, not like one I've ever seen. He jumps as high as a jackrabbit and has legs to match."

What a wonderful child she was. Her antics amused him. But how he wished he had gotten cleanly away from her. She would have been so much better off fending for herself at the soddy. He feared failing her. Having her along was a burden he wasn't sure he could shoulder.

"We'll shelter here the day, and cross the sands by night," he said. "You ought to try to get some sleep."

The abrupt tone puzzled her. The long harsh days on the trail had seeped all the funning right out of him. She hated that and wished for the old Reed back again.

The smile that died on her face put him to shame. "I guess I never realized how young you are, girl. I'm sorry about what happened back at the soddy. I never should have let it get that far."

She scowled fiercely. He looked so forlorn, she found herself regretting her earlier folly. At the same time she was unable to let his comment about her youth go unchallenged.

"Not too young to make you want me. Anyway, it wasn't your fault."

His harsh and bitter laugh frightened her. "No, you didn't make me. I do or don't do what I do. No one makes me. Or you, either, girl. Remember that, will you?"

Though she nodded, she was far from agreement. She had been made to do a lot of things in her young life, and she was sure that wasn't over with yet. 'You tried to make me go back home," she said with a pout.

"Yes, I suppose I did. But it was for your own good."

Hands tucked into the sagging waist of her overalls, she said with a distinct twinkle in her eye, "And what we did, that was for your own good. Mine, too, for that matter."

With that she trounced to where she had left her old felt hat on top of the pack of dwindling supplies. She crammed the dusty thing down on her head, picked up the pack, and headed for the sparse brush he had indicated for shade.

"Damn, girl, you are something," he murmured, but not loud enough for her to hear.

He would never forget the way she had made him feel when they held each other, her teasing because she didn't understand a man's needs. Such enjoyment of the basic human spirit was quite rare. Recalling their romp, he regretted his decision to keep his hands to himself, even though he knew it was the right one.

For three nights they walked. She was surprised at how much light the stars cast. A fingernail moon would appear in the western skies as they darkened, and before long she could see almost better than in the glaring light of day. Sedge, thorny cactus, and towering soap weed plants cast elongated shadows on the gleaming sand. He showed her how to eat the cactus fruit. Cutting open the spiny green leaves, he would dig out the meat and squeeze moisture into her mouth while she tilted her head back. The stuff tasted god-awful, right on the verge of being bitter, but by then she was finally convinced he knew more than she did. After all, they were still alive.

On the evening of the third day they came upon a cougar and her twin cubs.

The sun had dropped below the horizon, leaving a glorious orange sky behind. Strings of lavender-hued clouds lay like tattered lace along the horizon. She tramped behind him, chattering on about nothing in particular. The ground was smothered in darkness, so watching her feet made her stumble smack into his solid back.

He had scented the cat earlier and gone on the alert, saying nothing to her. Now he signaled her to be absolutely still. The female cougar, probably six to eight feet long and as tawny as the earth, was hunting. Stalking into the wind had kept her from catching the smell of humans.

Muscles bunched over her great shoulders, she approached her prey in slow motion. At first he couldn't see what the lioness saw, but he did see something else that clutched at his heart. A pair of cubs wrestled in a depression off to their right. He and Tressie had strayed inadvertently between the mother and her young. As long as the cat concentrated on the kill, they would be fine, but if she caught their scent, she would charge. He didn't want to shoot her and leave the cubs to die. Hell, he wasn't even sure he could hit her with the muzzle loader of hers.

Marksmanship was her forte, not his.

He motioned for her to crouch low and make herself smaller. She did and he held a finger to his lips. Green eyes wide, she nodded. Her heart hammered so loudly, the lion could surely hear it. Hugging both knees, she watched him finger a cap from the possible bag and ready the rifle for firing.

Why was he going to shoot such a gorgeous creature? Surely they couldn't eat it, and the cat was paying no attention to them at all. She wanted to shout a warning as the supple limbs of the beautiful animal propelled its lithe body forward inch by inch. She yelped when a rabbit erupted from nowhere and zigzagged across the prairie, the cat hot on its trail. Hunter and prey kicked up clouds of dust as they ran into the starlit night, zipping this way, then that through clumps of crackly sedge.

Soon there came a scream of pure terror such as she had never heard before. "Oh, God, what was that?"

He tapped her bowed head. "Hsst, be still and back up. Real slow." He almost stepped on her before she could make her trembling legs obey. Somehow getting to her feet, she scampered out of his way, ignoring his orders and clattering through the underbrush, kicking up rocks and debris.

The playing cubs, aroused by the noise, set up a burbling greeting, and he caught his breath.

"Stop," he said sharply, and lifted the barrel of the gun, sighting it as the cougar came in view, her limp kill hanging from strong jaws.

Tressie managed to quell her instinct to run, and did as he ordered. The cougar headed for her cubs, trotting so close by them, she could see the flash of golden eyes, smell her wild stench.

With a smothered sigh he carefully removed the cap from the rifle, letting the hammer down slowly. "Come on," he said, and headed on down the trail. He couldn't let her see how distraught he was.

Frozen to the spot, she watched, him stride away totally unable to follow. Her knees were shaking so badly she couldn't take that first step. She was going to be sick, and he could wait for her. After a moment, the feeling passed and she trotted to catch up.

Several mornings later, when she had begun to think the sand would go on forever, enormous jagged rocks appeared, protruding from the hot gritty soil like bizarre ships at sea. They settled in the welcome shade of one, a good place to spend the long hot day.

Reed pointed toward the distant western horizon at what looked like ragged clouds growing from the flat land. "There's Wyoming over yonder."

She strained to pick out what he saw. Her lips were dry; her mouth tasted as bitter as the cactus juice they'd lived on so long. The welcome sight of their destination perked her up considerably. This trip had already taken much longer than she had thought it would, and she was eager to reach the end.

"And then how far? How far to Bannack?"

He put an arm around her shoulder. "Ah, Tressie, girl. Let's just watch those mountains grow. That distance will be far enough to last us a long time. But isn't it good to see something besides sand and cactus?"

"Then how far to them?" She swept off her hat and took in the sight of the rugged peaks, hazy as they were. He was right. They were beautiful. She wiped at moisture forming in her eyes and sniffed. It had been a long time since she had cried.

"Ah, girl, I know what you mean." He took her in his

arms, resting his chin on top of her head. They had been together so long he felt attached to her in the way he supposed one would a family member. They had avoided physical contact, but it was mostly from exhaustion. Having made his secret vow of celibacy where she was concerned, he was glad of the harsh circumstance that robbed their bodies of energy. It made the vow easy to keep. She was still such a child and he a worthless deserter and coward, surely not worthy of her love.

She settled against his chest, welcomed the strength in his embrace and hugged him fiercely. The touch of his muscular body stirred something inside she could not identify, but supposed it was what Mama used to explain would be a female wanting. They were going to make it, and how wonderful that was. But she could not console herself with any attraction to Bannon. Papa had left them, deserted her and his pregnant wife, and he was no better a man, running like they all must, from responsibility. How could she consider giving her virginity to a man who wouldn't hesitate to leave her, who had tried once already?

Even as she pulled away, Reed found himself wanting her. Why was his body betraying him even while he argued the stupidity of such a thing? A man should have more control than that. Perhaps that's all it was, an animal lust. They had been alone together so very long. Once they made civilization, he could find him a fancy woman, get rid of all these desires the way a man was supposed to. That certainly didn't mean taking advantage of Tressie Majors while she was so vulnerable, and so young.

The endless land rolled to the mountains in huge waves that demanded struggling up and stumbling down. It was as if the dunes had turned into a grassy, turbulent ocean. On the morning of the third day with the coming dawn nudging their backsides, the mountains greeted them like walls of granite blotting out the sky. Huge boulders lay scattered about, and great arroyos cut scars into the red earth among a scraggly growth of greasewood and sage.

This day, as the sun climbed the metallic sky, he made no move to stop for their usual all-day sleep. For a while she trudged along at his heels, letting her thoughts wander. He spoke very little while they were on the move, and she had grown quite used to occupying her time with great fantasy voyages through fairy castles. But as the hours went by and he made no offer to stop, she grew tired of even those magical adventures.

Focusing on his ramrod-straight back where the shoulder strap of the possible bag cut across the blue flannel shirt, she muted a shout to stop. *Stop right here!* And then, quite abruptly, as if he'd heard her, he pulled up short.

She stumbled to a halt beside him. "What is it?"

"A wagon, just over yonder in the trees."

"Folks?" She peered where he pointed.

"Don't see anyone, but there's water there, too. You stay here while I check."

"I'm thirsty. Real honest-to-goodness water? Oh, I want to go, too."

He put an arm across her chest quite forcefully. "I said stay here, now do it."

The tone brooked no argument, and she heeded him, though doing so made her temper flare. He took the rifle with him and approached the covered wagon with a great deal of caution. One corner of the canvas whipped and snapped in the wind, and the tongue lay on the ground, empty of horse or oxen. No child cried, no human voice spoke. She smelled something on the wind, recognized blood and death, and began to tremble. Something or someone lay dead over there, and she was glad he had made her stay behind.

A few moments later he waved for her to join him. She

did so with a great deal of reluctance. He stood between her and the campsite.

"Just a woman and man here. They're dead. No need you looking. Climb up in the wagon and see if you can salvage anything. Take everything we can use. I'm going to…" He hesitated. "Never you mind what I'm going to do, just git yourself up there. Clothes, tools, vessels of any kind. Gather up everything. We'll take all we can carry."

"Did the Indians—?"

"Not now, girl. Not now." He turned her gently with a hand on each shoulder.

She climbed up and over the seat into the back of the wagon. If the Indians had done this, they hadn't bothered to raid, yet the pickings were very poor indeed. Obviously the family had begun with very little, or like so many had lightened their load as they went along until not much was left. There were some patchwork quilts and a blanket marked u.s. in one corner. She took those and added some plates, flatware, and two tin cups. There was no food. Hopping down from the tailgate, she added to her bundle a cooking vessel and a small hatchet.

A skin pouch beaded with moisture hung on the side of the wagon and her dry tongue caught at the roof of her mouth. Just a sip to hold her… there'd been nothing but liquid squeezed from cactus for so long. She pried out the stopper and took several languorous sips, rolling the last drops of cool water around in her mouth before swallowing. After she patted a handful over her face and neck, she gulped down some more.

She tied the corners of the Army blanket together, and Reed joined her, looking pale and sick. "I'll take that," he said. "There's a creek just yonder. We'll camp there tonight."

"So close to…?"

"I'm sorry, we'll go up stream a ways. That's as good as we can do. We need the water and neither of us can walk another step."

She sank gratefully on the banks of the bubbling creek when he chose a likely spot out of sight of the wagon. After drinking of the clear water, she removed her shoes, or what was left of them, and lowered her burning feet in the stream. With a sigh of contentment she lay back, one arm over her eyes.

He joined her, drank, and had just taken off a boot when she sensed his alarm and stiffened almost at the moment he hissed for silence.

She shifted, touched his arm.

"Shhh. Don't move."

The Indians had come back for them for sure. Don't move, indeed. All she could think was leap to her feet and run. She couldn't help it, every instinct screamed run and hide, fast.

"Stay still. I'll get the rifle."

She wouldn't run. She would not uncover her eyes. Every inch of her skin crawled until she itched with the need to flee. In her mind a towering, painted savage loomed over her. Did they hack away the scalp before or after they ravaged a woman?

Somewhere behind her the rifle went off with a tremendous *ka-whoom* that made the air thump against her eardrums. She screeched, he shouted, and she scrabbled as fast as she could into a stand of scrub nearby and hunkered down.

She heard him muttering, "Damn, damn, *damn*," but waited, afraid to breathe, open her eyes, or wiggle a toe.

After a second or two, "Tressie? Where the hell are you, girl? I think I got him. Could you go look?"

"In here," she squeaked, and waved a hand into the open. "You go look. I'm afraid." "Afraid of what, a dead deer? What are you doing in there? Oh, hell. You were right about that goddamned gun. Kicked the thunder out of me. Over there, girl, on the far bank, a mule deer. I think I hit him."

She crept from hiding to see him sprawled on his back rubbing at his shoulder. She ran to him. 'You okay?"

His grin was one of chagrin. "Got too excited, I guess. Let her kick the hell out of me. 'Course I'm okay. Git on over there. He might be on the move. Sometimes they do. Oh, Lord, can't you just taste the venison now? Hurry. I'm coming."

Without waiting for him to struggle to his feet, she high stepped it through the shallow creek, already imagining the juicy flavor of a venison steak roasted over hot coals.

Her experience at cleaning large game came in mighty handy that evening. Together they secured the swaying body to a good-sized tree branch and hoisted the young doe up by her hind legs. He produced a long-bladed knife, which she used to remove the musk gland from inside the rear leg. She slit open the belly of the deer with a precision that made him stare in wonderment.

"Lord, girl. Where'd you learn to do that?"

She shrugged, trying to act unconcerned, but inside she swelled with pride. It was time she carried her weight in this venture. "Go get the cooking vessel for the heart and liver, and you might as well build us a fire, too."

He threw her a cocky salute and marched off. They were both feeling pretty good, what with the prospect of a meal of fresh venison on top of their luck at finding water.

It was after dark before the meat was cooked. She sat at his side facing the fire, and with their fingers they ate chunky cuts of venison he sawed off with the shiny knife.

"Where'd you get the knife?" she asked.

"Off the dead man." He speared a hunk of meat.

The meat grew in her mouth. She gagged and made a valiant effort at swallowing the chunk of venison, but it wouldn't go down. Her stomach roiled. Hand over her mouth, she leaped up and ran for the woods, where she dropped to her knees and lost every bite of the delicious supper.

Moaning, she leaned against a tree and wiped her face. He followed her, his boots crunching through the leaves, and she felt ashamed. How foolish to be such a baby.

He knelt beside her, put an arm around her shoulders. "Too rich for you, I guess. Should have taken it easy. Ate too fast."

Let him think that if he wanted. It was better than the truth that she was just too queasy to handle eating from a dead man's knife blade.

He helped her up. "Come on, wash your face and get a drink. You can probably eat a little if you go slow and easy."

"I guess," she said, and went with him, but she was unable to eat any more of the venison. "Maybe tomorrow. Too bad it's so hot; the rest will spoil, I suppose."

He stirred and rose to his feet.

"Where you going?"

"I'm gonna make us some jerky to take along. We'll take a cut or two of the meat as well. We can eat on it till it grows hair, then start on the dried stuff. Half-rotten venison never hurt anyone, I don't suppose."

She had eaten her share of rotten meat. It was done when there was no other choice. That was just the way things were. She knew also that she would not suffer from her earlier revulsion again. It had been a momentary thing, brought about as much by eating too much rich meat on an empty stomach as anything.

In a few minutes he sloshed back across the creek carrying the other rear haunch from the mule deer. Squatting, he carved out a hefty chunk and began slicing around and around the piece of meat until he had a long, narrow, and unbroken strip of the purplish-red flesh. He spread it across the branches of a nearby fallen tree. Then he cut and laced green limbs together into a drying rack, which he propped so that the smoke from the fire would filter through it.

As he hung the meat, he said, "I don't do this as good as my grandmother, but it'll do. Now let's take a look at what you gleaned from the wagon."

Together they went through their windfall. The clothing was probably the most valuable find. Several pairs of britches and shirts, some woolen socks, a couple of full-skirted dresses, and a pair of bloomers. She had mixed emotions about someone else's tragedy being their saving grace.

"Why didn't the Indians take these?" she asked.

"Indians? It wasn't an Indian attack."

"What killed them? And what happened to their animals?"

He sharpened a small twig and picked at meat caught between his teeth. "Run off, I guess, or maybe a wandering band did take the animals. But I don't think so. They'd have taken the geegaws. The pots and clothes, this knife." He held up the blade, catching reflections from the fire that shot across the dark clearing.

She waited for him to explain the dead couple. The aroma of cooking meat hovered around the campsite as the wind laid for the night. From the dark tree branches, a dove cooed and settled in. A distant owl added to the night songs Still he kept his silence.

"What killed them?" she finally asked.

"A sickness," he said real low.

"Oh, God," She clutched a pair of socks under her chin, ran her fingers over the quilt she'd spread out to sit on. A quilt that had once covered those two poor souls buried in a strange land with no family to mourn their passing. Where had they come from? Did someone back home envision their loved ones living in the promised land? Suppose she and Reed caught the disease. How dreadful.

She cleared her throat, dropped the socks, and got up. An early waxing moon appeared with languid grace and spread a mantle of silver across the land.

He glanced at her, his eyes gleaming unspoken questions she was afraid had no answers. At least not any she could give.

Rather than try, she whispered huskily, "I have to take a bath. No snakes this time, please. Just come with me." She reached down toward him, felt a great rush of being safe as his hand closed over hers and he rose to his feet beside her.

Five

Reed sat on the bank to remove his boots, watching Tressie as if in a trance. What they were about to do was wrong, but he could no more stop himself than he could wish the golden moon out of the night sky into her arms. And the way she focused those moss-green eyes so deliberately on him, he knew she felt the same. It was like falling off a cliff. After the final step there would be no going back and nothing to grab hold of, and they had both made that step. He had no idea what had changed between them, what had removed the barriers. Maybe they just needed to celebrate being alive.

She kicked off her shoes and took his hand. Even now, after he'd removed his boots, she feared he would back away from her. Together they waded into the cold water fully clothed. The stream bed was littered with smooth stones, some slick with moss. She grabbed at his arm to keep from falling.

Near a cutback of gravel, the unceasing flow of water had hollowed out a basin in the bedrock, and they came together there. The gentle rush of the whispering stream caressed her breasts. With trembling hands he cupped them in the palms of his hands.

Soon it would be too late to stop this. She was a child. Women married younger than this. The arguments leaped through his mind. He wanted her, but it might be only because they were so alone out here and he hadn't touched a woman in so long. With an enormous sigh, he bent to her, lips slightly parted. She met the kiss with lips that trembled. The mountains and the rising moon watched; the water murmured softly.

His hands swept upward to unhitch the galluses of the overalls she wore, and they slipped off. His fingers fumbled with the buttons of her shirt, and she enfolded his hands in hers. Inching back, she slowly raised her eyes to meet his gaze. He brushed at her cheek, a question in the dark eyes.

She nodded. "Let me," she said, and began to undo his shirt, finally skinning it off his shoulders. The sinewy curves of his arms and chest gleamed in the moonlight. With trembling fingers she combed the black locks away from one side of his angular face and kept her hand there, entwined.

"Girl, we ought not to do this," he said, turned to bury his lips in her palm as if hoping she would disagree. His breath was warm, his tongue raspy against her skin.

"I know. I'm afraid." She hunched into his embrace, arms folded protectively over her young breasts, trusting him to do what was right. But how the hell did he know what right was? Certainly not taking advantage of this sweet, innocent young girl.

Bodies water-slicked to a petal softness, they eased into an embrace. Both sighed, then cried out in their ecstasy of coming together. Up on the bank the fire crackled, and a whiff of smoke curled their way.

He tasted of her deeply, the flesh of her shoulders, throat, chin, ears. She felt him rise against her and knew that this time their lovemaking would be for real, not some fumbling attempt by a wounded man and a desperate girl. He wanted her. She could feel the urgency of his desire down to the fingertips of his broad hands kneading at her back. A heated passion cloaked them safely in an imaginary cocoon.

Hands spanning her waist, he lifted her out of her overalls, holding her close. She locked her legs around his waist, their bodies molding together as if they had long ago been cut from one piece and were at last being put back together.

He tried to be easy with her and the sharp pain of penetration faded as he waited for her to relax. She cried out and began to move with him so he could tell it was all right. The water cradled them; the moon and stars looked on.

Buried in her warm sweetness, he carried her from the creek. Kicking his britches from around both ankles, he knelt on the quilt beside the fire.

Tumbling, their gleaming limbs tangled in the throes of passion. Her lithe young body begged for more. In her first love's passion and loneliness, she reached into the very soul of the man who had saved her from death. She would keep him with her always. Him and only him. Gone was all memory of the very reason they were together in this wilderness. Gone the fears and doubts.

They slept wrapped together, naked limbs entwined like young animals.

He awoke just at dawn, but couldn't arise without disturbing her. She slept soundly, making soft purring noises with each breath. So he lay there, one arm trapped under her head, thighs pinned by one of her legs.

He considered the possibility of simply carrying her away with him. Heading in the opposite direction, away from Bannack. And then what? Some soldier would find them, or he would spot a familiar face, and be off like the coward he was. He had absolutely nothing to offer her. He'd been a wanderer all his life, turning tail and running at the first sign of trouble. Her father had been like that. Why complicate things further?

He sensed her watching him and looked to see sleep-smoked green eyes.

"You look sad," she said, putting the tip of one finger to his chin. "What is it?"

Unwinding, he tossed his head so that dark hair tumbled into his eyes.

She watched him shove it back impatiently, and sensed his withdrawal, his uncertainty. "What's wrong?" she sat up. The quilt fell from her naked breasts, but she ignored that. The bereft look on his face warned her that something was wrong; she just couldn't figure out what.

"I'm sorry about...about last night."

"Sorry?" she echoed, a pain growing down in her chest.

He nodded, turned away from the sweet beauty of her. "Put some clothes on." His voice sounded rougher than he had intended and he regretted the tears that sprung to her eyes.

Disappointment turned to anger and she scrambled away, dragging the pack of clothing with her into the brush. She chose a dress salvaged from the wagon of the dead family. If she died, then she died. What did it matter, anyway? Reed was going to run, first chance he got. She could see it in his eyes.

The chambray dress hung loosely and dragged on the ground so that she had to lift the skirt to stomp barefoot into the clearing. He wasn't going to do this to her! She'd given him her own true self, something no other man had had. Wisely, he had made himself scarce so she couldn't tell him so. Just like a man.

By the time he returned, her initial fury had turned into a somber pout and she did her best to ignore him.

He held up a dripping wad of clothing. "Found these washed up on the bank down the creek a ways, but they'll dry." He sorted out her overalls and his shirt, hanging them on the low limbs of a tree. "Sorry about your shirt. It must have washed away."

She glared at him. How could he be so casual about something that had meant so much to her? They had made love, and she would always treasure the memory. He seemed more concerned about their clothes. Was he really just a rounder, a thief or worse?

He studied her face, pretty even when she drew it up in such a fierce frown. This wasn't going to be easy. Like most young women, she wanted what she wanted, and worried about the consequences later, if at all. Right now, he supposed she wanted him. Well, he wanted her, too, but had a little better sense about it than she did. One day she would thank him.

Meanwhile, he tried to lighten the mood. "You look like a little girl in her mother's clothes," he said, and laughed when she tossed her head and stumbled on the hem of the dress in her haste to turn away. "We'll stay here a day or two before heading into the mountains. Rest up."

"Whatever you say," she snapped.

And that's the way it went that day and the next. They spent their nights sleeping apart on opposite sides of the fire. She was glad when he told her they would leave the next morning.

Traveling with his silences was much easier than remaining in one place with them.

She arose early the morning they were to leave, dressed hastily in pants and shirt, and prepared johnnycakes for breakfast. They ate in total silence, each avoiding the other's gaze. He busied himself with the packs they would carry, and she took the water pouch to the creek.

Dumping what was left of the water—it had tasted brackish and old—she rinsed the container thoroughly before immersing it in the crystal stream. Bubbles floated to the surface, making small gurgling noises as the container filled. After fitting in the stopper, she lay the pouch safely on the bank and leaned forward to drink deeply. The icy sweet liquid tasted better than the finest apple cider or grape squeezings Grammy ever produced.

The craggy mountains cut into the indigo morning sky. The air smelled vaguely of granite and soil and pine forests, all tinged with the sweet smoke from their campfire. Arching her back, she stretched both arms, then ran the flat of her hands over her unbound breasts. Fingers curled loosely in her lap, she thought she could feel him there still, deep in that dark and wonderful secret place, all hot and wet and sweet. Pulses of desire kicked through her and she closed her eyes a moment. Damn him for making her feel so good and then turning away.

Reed hung back in the trees and quietly watched Tressie for a moment. The sight of her took his breath away. The pale golden light of early morning and the ugly clothing blurred her shape, but he could imagine each soft curve as if she wore nothing. She appeared as unreal as a dream. He smothered a desire to go to her, hold her close, tell her how he felt. It was no use, and he shook his head vigorously. What a fool he was. Wanting a woman he couldn't have because he didn't have the good sense to be a real man.

The sun continued its climb into the sky, and it was time they left. With an impatient backward glance, he returned to the campsite. Angry at his own weaknesses, he strapped on the bulkier of the two packs he had fashioned from the Army blanket. He would carry that plus his heavily laden saddlebags and the rifle.

Tressie surveyed the larger pack on his back while she pulled on socks and shoes. "I can carry my own weight." She hefted the smaller one and grunted. "Ooof, it's heavy."

He squinted at her. At least she was speaking to him again. "They both are; mine's just lumpier. We'll take turns with the water pouch. That suit you?" His eyes sparked a questioning glance in her direction.

"I suppose. What's that smell?"

"Well, it ain't me. I bathed with you, remember?"

She ignored his teasing. It wasn't going to be that easy to get back in her good graces.

They'd done a lot more than bathe, but he obviously wanted to forget that. "It smells like rotten meat."

"Not yet it ain't. It'll go over quick, but we can eat on it awhile. You've got it in your poke. Sorry, it just worked out that way. Once it starts to making us sick, we'll leave it for the varmints."

She screwed up her face.

"It beats starving, girl, and I didn't come this far to do that. That's pretty desolate country yonder." He swung an arm toward the slopes of the craggy mountains. "Nothing much lives there that's fit to eat."

Neither is rotten deer meat, but she didn't speak her thought. He'd kept them alive this long. "What about the water? Will this be enough?" She held up the leather pouch with its wide shoulder strap.

"It'll have to be. It'll get heavy. We'll trade it off if you need to. Or, if you can't handle it, I'll take it."

She jutted her jaw at him, dropped the wide belt over her head, and snugged the pouch under the opposite arm. He had to help her shrug into the loops he'd fashioned and adjust the blanket pack. He tried not to touch any part of her, not the satiny soft skin nor the downy wisps of gleaming red hair.

While he was kicking sand over the smoldering camp-fire, she heard him mutter, "Stubborn little colt," in a tone she thought to be regretful.

She soon learned why he had insisted on a two-day stay to rest up before beginning their journey into the rugged foothills. Even when the land appeared flat the going was rough.

Once she remarked about that feeling and he laughed uproariously. "From here on out, everything's uphill. And if it's not, that's only because you're fixing to really climb."

Fear of the unknown made it impossible for her to remain coldly aloof for long. He was her protector if not her lover. They were, after all, the only humans within hundreds of miles. Or so she hoped. It was hard not to imagine savage Indians around every bend.

They stopped to rest when the sun was high. As they sat against an outcropping of enormous boulders to chew on tough jerky, she asked, "Have you been out here before? I mean, because you seem to be so easy about everything."

He contemplated her question for a long time, as he always did. Staring off at the distant snow-capped peaks, he watched the young boy in his memories, mounted and riding faster than the prairie winds. Black hair flying, heels locked against the horse's sides, lithe body a part of the animal he rode. The Sioux were the finest horsemen alive. No one could best them. Once, not many years ago, he had heard a general call the Sioux "the greatest light cavalry in the world." How he wished he had a horse now.

He tossed his head and sharpened the images of the mountains to blot out those of so long ago. Those days, like all the others to follow, were gone forever. He no longer thought like an Indian, if he ever had. Perhaps there was no place for him, for he found life in the white world equally impossible.

He swung his head around finally and stared back the way they had come to answer her question. "Spent some time around Fort Laramie, but it was a long time ago, before I decided I was man enough to go east to help fight that crazy war. 'Course things here ain't changed much yet. They will, though, once folks get their minds off fighting and start moving west." He chewed thoughtfully. "No man will ever tame these mountains, though. Even the Indian makes of them sacred ground so they have good reason for not coming here."

"Then why don't we go on down to the Oregon Trail? It'd be a lot easier."

"We're headed to Grasshopper Creek, and that's north of here. North of Fort Laramie, too. No sense in going down to that place. You wouldn't like it anyway. We'll get through all right. Lots of men have. Special kinds of men. Mountain men, trappers, Indian holy men, the like. I got just enough of all kinds in me to see us through. Don't worry."

It was clear she might never find out why he shied away from any place there might be people. She herself wouldn't have minded visiting civilization once in a while.

Seeing snow on the higher mountain peaks surprised her, for it was most surely July by now. What would this country be like come winter? She prayed she wouldn't have to find out, but wondered if they would ever reach their destination.

Soon they began to spot enormous boulders layered one upon the other like peculiar growths. He pointed out copper-colored brush—mountain mahogany, he said—that grew in profusion. Once again he made cactus a part of their diet.

She never managed to consume the rank-flavored juice without making a face. It had such an odd, gingery flavor. Not at all like ginseng or sassafras tea.

"Swallow as much as you can," he said when she puckered her lips shut. "It's good for you. You won't take the blackleg."

She did as he told her, regarding him with renewed respect. "What's the blackleg?" she asked, wiping her lips and watching him tilt back his head to drip the liquid into his open mouth.

"It's what happens when you don't eat enough cactus juice."

"Silly. I meant, do your legs really turn black?"

"Yep, after you suffer all sorts of other awful things. You get sores all over, you can't be up and around no time without wearing plumb out, and finally your legs turn black."

"Then what happens?" He surely was teasing her, though she did know that there were some dreadful maladies just waiting to strike down perfectly healthy folks.

"You die," he said, and gulped down the final squeezings. Tear spurted from her eyes, and he quickly changed the subject.

"Longer we stay out here, the hairier we get." He pulled his long hair into a tail at the back of his head and tied it with a length of rawhide. "Might need to get haircuts, both of us." He rubbed at the full-blown beard. "Was I pure Indian, I wouldn't have to worry about growing face hair like this."

Tears forgotten, she dodged and laughed when he tousled her own wild locks. Despite the funning though, she couldn't forget what he'd said about black leg. She didn't want to die of anything, and certainly not something that turned your legs black. From then on she'd drink the foul cactus juice every day.

The next night, following a grueling day of climbing after which he complained that they had only made five miles, she awoke with cramps in her stomach, a swimming head, and burning with fever. No change of position eased the pain. She felt as if she were lying on one of those craggy outcroppings they'd struggled over the day before. Fear that she had the dreaded black leg disease made her numb with terror. She lay in total misery the rest of the night, alternately shivering with cold and burning up. When the cramps intensified, she stuffed a fist into her mouth to keep her moaning from awakening him.

At dawn he wandered away from camp to relieve himself. When he came back, he called out. "Up and at 'em, girl."

"I can't. Oh, I hurt." She shifted and groaned.

He knelt beside her and touched the back of his hand to her forehead. His dark eyes clouded and he stared off into the distance. *Dear Lord, don't let it be*, he prayed silently.

"I'll be okay," she whispered. "Just let me rest is all. Probably that old cactus juice, or that stinking deer meat."

He met her feeble attempt at humor with a solemn stare and a shake of his head.

Hit by another bout of intensely sharp pains, she grasped her stomach and cried out. Gazing up into his rugged features, which were wrinkled in concern, she imagined the sensual visage when they'd made love. Smilng at her, fine lips moving in silent words, dark eyes swimming with desire. She reached up a trembling hand, cupped the bearded jaw, and gasped, "Oh, Reed, I've missed you so. Where have you been?" The welcome darkness swallowed her, but his name followed her into its depths.

He caught at the small hand and held it to his lips. They hadn't made love since leaving the creek campsite. Harsh reality kept coming between them. But neither had spoken of it since their argument down by the river. She looked so frail. God, he hoped she didn't die.

He had to get her to shelter of some kind where he could take care of her properly. She could have cholera, which was almost always fatal. Still he had seen people live through it. No matter what, he had to try. So he fashioned a travois of birch and alder, bound her and the supplies to it, and stepped into the harness.

She lapsed into a frightening world where she pursued a man who looked and sounded like Papa, until he turned around to reveal fangs and drooling lips, head as bald as river stones. At times, when she was rational, there would be cool water on her brow and at her lips. She occasionally awoke to a jarring that bruised her down to the bone. Strapped into some kind of contraption, she was being dragged along. Once she remembered screaming for Papa to help her. Oh, how she needed him to save her from this torturous treatment, take her back home to Missouri so she could see Mama again.

All day he pulled the heavy travois. He pulled until every muscle ached, until his vision was clouded with weariness. All the while he searched for a place where he could keep her cool and sheltered from the elements. Nights in the mountains were often wet and frigid. Sudden summer storms could drench the countryside. Before he found the trapper's cabin, he had begun to think he was back in the war. He began to have visions of stumbling through the dead and dying, heard their pitiful cries for mercy. Even when he spotted the cabin, his thinking had become so muddled from exhaustion that at first he saw no way to get her to it.

The crude shack clung to an outcropping on a trail that appeared to lead straight up the mountain's face. Its back into the bluffs, the cabin formed a fort of sorts, a place in which to stand off marauding man or beast. Despite its inaccessibility, the poor structure had four walls and a roof. Just what he needed if he were to save Tressie's life.

Water was another thing he would need, and a spring flowed beside the path, obviously born of snow melt high up in the mountains.

He set down the travois gently. For a long while he stood there, stooped and contemplating, bringing himself back to full reality. He couldn't drag the travois up the narrow goat trail; it was too hazardous. He would have to carry her and all the supplies, which would mean at least three trips up and down the treacherous path. He was exhausted, spent to the point of collapse. Would this be where he finally failed this young woman he scarcely knew?

From somewhere behind the mountain peak, thunder rumbled in ominous persistence. The breeze shifted, turned colder. He had to get her up there now. Before it rained. Failure could result in her death, something he wasn't willing to face.

Stumbling to her side, he untied the strips of rawhide he'd laced over her and the quilt wrappings.

She rolled her head, murmured, "Mama…Papa."

He touched her skin with the back of his hand. Burning up! He tried not to think that she was calling for another man who had failed her. After two awkward attempts, he managed to lift her while keeping the quilt over her feverish, frail body. In his arms she seemed so tiny and helpless, and he became terrified of losing her, of standing helplessly by while the disease snatched her away. He didn't consider that she wasn't his to lose.

"Ah, Tressie," he whispered, eyes stinging with unshed tears. Her head tucked under his chin burned a fiery spot in his flesh.

A gust of cold, wet wind danced around the edges of the mountain crags, hitting him full in the face as he began his climb. He had to go slowly, placing each foot and testing the safety before taking his next step. If he started to slip, nothing would stop the both of them from tumbling over the precipice.

Rocks shifted and spilled from the edge of the trail, and he could no longer see his feet in the falling darkness. Time and again he had to stop and rest, leaning elbows against the steep incline to keep from dropping her. He tried to think of happier times, better times, but what haunted him were her huge eyes the way they had looked early that morning when she awoke and told him she was sick. They'd been filled with a fear he'd never seen there before. Not even the day they forded the Loup had she looked so scared. She thought she was going to die, and he couldn't let that happen.

One more step and he reached the cutback in the rocks where the cabin slouched. He fell against the sagging plank door and went to his knees inside, clutching her in desperation. The cabin was worse than he had thought. He had hoped for something in occasional use by a mountain trapper, but what he found was a deserted hovel. It stank of the droppings of various tenants. He had to chase out a family of pack rats. All other occupants had flown or fled with the opening of the door.

He had no choice but to lay her on the floor. He would bring up the rest of their supplies, then he could get the place cleaned up enough to fashion her a bed near a crude mud fireplace at the back of the hut. He kicked away some rubble and lowered her gently, being careful to cover her before going down for the packs.

The next time she regained consciousness it was to the view of a cobwebbed roof. She tried to turn her head and look around, but the slightest movement caused her head to pound thunderously. She squeezed her eyes shut and lay very still until the waves of pain passed.

Swallowing tentatively, she opened one eye and let out a feeble croak, calling out to she knew not who.

A great shadow shut off the glare of sunlight pouring in the doorway and she covered her eyes with one hand to avoid the monster of her nightmares. A far-off cry came to her ears. Who had made that feeble sound? Was it the child? He needed nursing, and Mama was— "Mama, oh, Mama, ooo."

With one trembling hand she fumbled between her breasts, intending to unbutton her dress, but there was nothing but bare skin under a thin quilt. A warm wet cloth lay over her abdomen. She shoved the covers down with the flats of her hands, baring both breasts.

"No, don't die. The baby's coming. See him? You mustn't die. Who will feed the baby?"

Reed stood in the doorway a moment longer, then crossed the room to her side. A blinding shaft of sunlight threw his features into shadow as he approached the bed where she lay. He wanted to gather her into his arms, but instead dropped to his knees, and with gentle fingers pulled the quilt up to cover her breasts. He remembered tasting of those lovely nipples, rosy, sweet, and burning with passion.

She licked at dry, split lips. They stung. "Papa? Have you seen Papa?"

Sadly he shook his head, produced a water-soaked cloth and moistened her mouth. 'You're gonna be okay, I promise."

She remembered then in a rending flash like lightning crashing across the prairie. "Reed?

Where are we? What happened to me?"

Instead of answering her questions, he rose and went across the room to ladle her a bowl of broth from a simmering pot.

Sitting on the floor beside her, he blew on the spoonful of steaming liquid, then tilted drops into her mouth. After a few swallows, she clamped her lips and turned her head away.

"Good, that was good," he said, and wiped her mouth carefully. "You'll take more later."

Despite all the unanswered questions, she dropped off to sleep. When she awoke again, darkness had closed in around the cabin, lit only by a small fire at the hearth. She was alone, and that frightened her terribly. It would be better to run away and hide somewhere, but she was too weak to get out of bed. She rubbed the palms of her hands over her cool skin. Naked. Naked under the covers. Who had taken off her clothes? And where was everybody? Mama, Papa?

No, *Reed*.

Reed Bannon, the man who'd dragged her across the high plains and saved her life as she' d once saved his.

The sound of his voice, his words falling soft and gentle on her soul, came as if through a dream. She recalled with sweet clarity the night they had made love. The water cold, their desire hot. His mouth warm and moist. His hardness so gently breaking the shell of her womanhood.

Then nothing. He hadn't touched her again, despite them being thrown together in bath and bed night after night on the long trek. Tears leaked from the corners of her eyes, as if she were mourning a great loss.

Very carefully she rolled her head to look toward the door. Crude skins of some kind hung over the opening that earlier had been uncovered. Except for the glow from a small fire it was dark in the room.

Without a sound to warn of his coming, Reed pushed the skins aside and came in. She bit at the back of her hand to keep from screaming.

"Awake again? Hungry?" he asked.

"You were gone. I was afraid."

Though her voice was stronger, it still didn't really sound like her own.

"Nonsense," he admonished, and dipped out another bowl of soup, this time adding a few chunks to the broth. "Since when are you afraid of anything, Tressie Majors?"

Something about the curt tone in his voice warned her that things weren't as they had been before her illness, but she didn't catch on right away. She ate the entire bowl of soup.

"Think you can get up?" he asked when she had finished.

She tried to lift her arms and legs, shook her head. Not possible, too weak.

"Then I'll carry you," he said, and scooped her from the bed, quilt and all. "We're gonna get some of the stink blowed off you," he told her, and she heard the grin in his words, though she couldn't see his face.

He was the same after all. Tressie locked her arms firmly around his neck. Outside the door she gulped in a deep breath and gazed around at glistening stars in the vast purple-velvet sky. Far to the west hung a sliver of moon, so thin and fine as to be almost invisible. Cradled in its curve rested a bold star.

"Look at that," he said, turning so she could see it better. "Old man moon holding that bright young'un safe and sound. He'll come to no harm, I'd wager."

He lowered his head and made a choking sound down deep in his throat, and she felt the heat of his breath through the quilt on her bare flesh. Goose bumps raised and she tightened her thin arms around his neck.

He breathed in the scent of her illness, which was driven back now, defeated. She would not die, and he'd wager she would want a bath soon. The notion made him grin despite his sorrow at losing her to something stronger than cholera.

"Better get you back inside, girl. Just wanted you to see the world didn't go anywhere while you were away."

He had her back in bed before she asked, "How long? How long was I sick?"

"I kept track of the days, scratched 'em on the wall there." He grinned his full and familiar grin. "Somehow knew you'd want to know. Let's see here, there's five, six, eight marks all told. 'Course I didn't start them till I got you here, and that took all of a day and into the night. Reckon that makes nine or ten days and nights of fever." He turned his back on her for a moment and pawed at the floor with one foot. "I thought you were going to die there for a while." Then he faced her. "Should have known better than that, though, girl. You are tough as rawhide."

"What was it, do you know? Not blackleg?" She couldn't keep the quivering from her own voice.

"No, girl. Not that. Can't know for sure, without a doctor, but I'd say you had cholera, bad as it was."

Tressie clenched both hands over her mouth. "A miracle I'm still alive. You saved my life, you surely did."

"It was the water. I should have known better when we found them folks and buried them. Taking their water pouch… stupid, stupid. I plain didn't think. They must of got some bad water on their travels, some was still in the pouch, and we just filled it from the blamed creek and come on. That's the only way I can account for it. I burned the blamed thing in the fire."

Though her eyelids fluttered closed, she struggled to watch Reed longer. The way he paced when agitated, the way he threw his hair back from his face before gazing at her. He was looking more and more like the Indian that he was. His mother's tribe, the Dakota Sioux, had left their mark on him. She wanted to listen to the deep vibrating tones of his voice, lulling her into a security she'd never known with anyone else. But she couldn't stop the blackness from descending. This night she slept without dreams that she could recall and awoke feeling a great cleanness deep in her chest.

After breakfast he took her outside again, this time leaving her on a huge boulder near the cabin while he refreshed her sickbed. After he went back inside, she unfolded the quilt and exposed her pale naked body to the warmth of the morning sun. She could then take in their surroundings, and what she saw made her gasp in wonderment. At her feet, stretching for miles, lay the country over which they had traveled. Cactus and golden and copper scrub and scraggly pine scattered amid building-sized boulders. A narrow and steep path with a treacherous drop along one side led up to the cabin. And at their back door rose the majestic mountains. All purples and blues and umbers, capped by a pure white snow that glistened brazenly in the warm summer sun.

Heat from the sun's rays lulled her and she leaned back on her arms, closing her eyes. He came upon her like that, and studied every curve and line of her before he spoke, trying to memorize them for later when they parted.

"Are you tired yet?" he finally asked, startling her into a tiny squeak of surprise. He gazed, as she had earlier, out across the vast panorama, a look of pure wonderment on his face.

"You frightened me," she whispered when she realized her bare body was exposed to him, if he cared to look.

"I didn't mean to. You ought to...I think it would be a good idea if you...Aw, hell, I'll just go back inside and leave you be till you're ready to come in. And would you put that dang thing over yourself before you call me back out here?"

She watched him go, glanced down at her bony white body, and giggled. Not much there to look at, that was for sure.

That night she sat wrapped in the quilt, knees drawn up under her chin. "Could we stay here awhile? It's so nice having a roof and walls and a door. I can turn over in my bed without worrying about laying on a rattler or a scorpion."

He shrugged, sitting cross-legged nearby. "No matter to me. You won't be fit to travel for a spell yet. It's you wants to find your Papa, not me. I got no place in particular to go."

"Why is that?" she asked.

"Why is what?"

"Why is it that you have no place to go? Why did we cross country in the wilds like we did, instead of going on down to the Platte and the Oregon Trail? You still scared of the Army?"

"'Course not, girl. Don't be foolish. I just don't like people. See what happened to us when we come upon some that had already passed on? You come down with a sickness. Happens every time. Folks carry all kinds of sickness of the mind and body and spirit. Man's better off alone."

"Well, a woman ain't. A woman likes company."

"You got company."

She nodded and smiled at him. "And you're not alone."

He rose effortlessly, not uncrossing his ankles until he stood upright. Be damned if he was going to do what he was aching to do. Take that little girl in his arms and... But he couldn't even think of such.

"And I think tomorrow you better put you on some clothes. Now that you're feeling so pert and sassy." He got out of there fast. No sense tempting fate.

She didn't take well to Reed's leaving her to her own devices, in fact was downright angry about it. She fussed around the cabin, decided to air the bedding and the spare clothing, and was unrolling Reed's meager belongings when she found the exquisite deerskin pouch. It was wrapped carefully in brown paper and tied with a thong. Curiosity immediately got the best of her. And besides, he shouldn't have taken off like he did. Serve him right if she got nosy.

On unwrapping it Tressie gasped and gently touched her cheek to the velvety feel of the fine leather. It smelled of tobacco and another elusive fragrance not unlike apples. An intricate beadwork design decorated one side of the small pouch, and stitched into the bottom were the initials RB, followed by a very unusual set of marks similar to a cattle brand in the vague shape of a tepee overcast by an arrow.

Tressie studied the small pouch, but could only guess at its significance. Probably belonged to Reed's Sioux mother, but why his initials. Perhaps she had fashioned it for him. But Reed said he had left the Sioux before his thirteenth birthday. Could he have carried this throughout all those years and even during the war, keeping it so well preserved?

She loosened the top and looked inside. Empty. How very curious. With a great deal of care she rewrapped the deerskin pouch in its brown paper and replaced the thong, trying to tie it in the precise same way. This was obviously something very important to him, and she tucked it back where she'd found it.

As soon as she exhausted the few cleaning chores around the cabin she began to explore the surrounding terrain. He continued to remain away from the cabin during the daylight hours, giving her plenty of time. During the forays she wore men's britches and shirts because of their comfort and the ease with which she could scramble around on the goat trails.

She was thusly dressed, her disreputable old hat crammed over her mop of hair, when she stepped around a sharp curve in the lower trail that led away from the cabin, right into the path of an Indian woman astride a small horse. Before Tressie could turn tail and run, a man's voice boomed out at her.

"You stay put, mister, or you'll be dealing with the wrath of the Lord. Move even to blink, and I'll blow your head clean off."

Tressie did exactly as the voice ordered. She stayed put.

Six

If the Indian woman astride the pony hadn't put an end to the standoff by letting out the most godawful holler, Tressie might have remained fixed to that same spot for an eternity. She had no wish to have her head blown off, and even if she might have chanced that, she was frozen stiff with fear. But the shrill ululating cry that came from the squaw sent Tressie kicking up dirt in a speedy retreat. She couldn't help running from the savage noise, even though all the while she expected a ball from the unseen man's gun to smash into the back of her head.

Running like mad, she fetched up at the cabin, made a wide, almost uncontrolled turn, and threw herself inside. Seeking the darkest corner, she huddled there and listened. It was impossible to control her harsh breathing. Most surely the wild man would hear and blow her to hell, as promised.

After a while, when nothing happened, she reined in her galloping imagination. He'd mistaken her for a man. Maybe if she hurried and put on a dress he wouldn't kill her.

No, of course not. Not right away. First he'd ravage her. She shuddered and hugged herself.

He must be as big as a grizzly by the sound of his voice. And where was Reed, anyway? The very idea, leaving her all alone out here in this wilderness to face such dangers as wild Indian women and their giant protectors.

Just as she summoned up enough courage to creep to the door and take a look around, she heard laughter, the soft plodding of a horse, and men's voices. Though they came closer, the words remained indistinguishable. Some kind of foreign lingo. The woman said something rather curtly and two men laughed. Two men?

Tressie catapulted across the cabin and raced outside. There stood Reed with an apparition nearly twice his size, head covered all over in hair and fur. Both talking as calm as you please, sizing each other up, like men do on first meeting.

Relieved to learn she would not be shot, Tressie threw herself between the two, choosing as a target the large stranger.

She kicked out at his stump-sized legs. "He tried to kill me."

"Whoa, lad," the man boomed. With a palm wide as her girth, he held fast to the top of her head so that she flailed away at thin air.

"I'm not a lad." Tressie kept swinging.

Reed wrapped an arm around her waist and dragged her out of reach of the man. The Indian woman, who had dismounted from the pony during the fracas, watched in stoic silence, hands clasped under a tremendous belly.

"Behave yourself, Tressie," Reed grated into her ear. "Come on, now, he didn't know you meant no harm. Cool off. You'll hurt yourself."

Dizzy and tired out, she slumped over his arm and gasped for air. He was right. She felt her knees go all wobbly and was grateful that Reed supported her, otherwise she would have fallen flat on her face.

"Okay, that's better," he said, but kept the arm around her nevertheless. "It's okay, Dooley, you're safe now. She's tamed."

"A real hellcat, ain't she?" Dooley said. "And to think I mistook her for a lad." Both men laughed uproariously.

If Tressie hadn't been totally winded, she would have taken them on, one at a time or together. As it was, she settled for glaring at the man Reed called Dooley.

He surely had a face under that dusty-colored hair somewhere. From the noise he made there had to be a mouth in there. Eyes, too, since he obviously could see. He wore a most disreputable outfit: wide-legged pants stuffed down in tall black boots, and a long-tailed jacket, under which there was a sweat-soaked white shirt gone to gray. Why did he wear the jacket if he was hot enough to sweat? He carried the longest rifle she'd ever laid eyes on.

"Your woman, I take it," Dooley bellowed. "Kind of peculiar in the eyes of the Lord to see a woman so clothed."

"What do you care?" Tressie gasped.

"Madame, if I hadn't lost my hat over a ravine just this very morning, I'd take it off to you for your sheer spunk."

The broad-faced Indian woman tugged at Dooley's jacket tail and said something in that peculiar tongue that Tressie had heard earlier.

"She wants to know if they can stay here the night," Reed muttered in Tressie's ear. "What do you think?"

"And get scalped in my sleep? And how do you know what she's saying, anyway?"

"She's Sioux. And not apt to scalp either of us, or anyone else, for that matter."

Tressie met the sloe-eyed stare of the beautiful young woman. Challenging yet anxious. She smiled and turned on Dooley with distrust. "What about him?"

"He says he's a trapper recently called to the cloth."

"What?" Tressie twisted to peer into Reed's face. "He's a trapper and a preacher?"

Reed nodded. "What he says."

"On my way to the gold camps to carry the merciful healing

of our Lord to those poor hardworking souls lost to their Creator," Dooley bellowed.

"Sounds like a preacher, all right," Tressie told Reed, as yet unwilling to directly address the bear of a man.

"Well, then, we can surely extend our hospitality, considering this place don't really belong to us anyways. Dooley could just exercise his rights and toss us out."

Tressie gritted her teeth. "Rights? What rights?"

"The rights of the biggest and strongest," Reed answered under his breath.

Tressie contemplated heading for the cabin and the Kentucky rifle. "Just let him try. I'll equalize things."

"Whoa, now, girl. You've had just about all the excitement you need for one day," Reed said with a chuckle. "Dooley, let's just all go inside and we'll stir up a little something for supper. You're welcome, both of you. Ain't they, Tressie?"

Having caught a second wind, she pulled free from his grasp. "I reckon," she grumbled. "But I hope they have something to add to the pot. He looks like he could eat himself a full- grown bear without burping."

Dooley roared with laughter. "I'd like to know where you got this little gal. Seems she's a match for just about anyone."

"He didn't get me, Mr. Dooley. I got him. You tell your wife she's welcome to come inside and rest a bit, would you?"

Reed spoke softly to the woman, and the words sounded like the trilling of music. He turned to her, eyes alight. "Her name is Bitter Leaf," he said as if presenting Tressie with a new treasure. "And she's going to have a child pretty quick."

"I can see that." In spite of her sharp tone, Tressie sympathized with his enjoyment of being among one of his own. He might be a little proud of his Indian heritage despite claims to the contrary.

Tressie took Bitter Leaf's arm and guided her inside the

cabin. She was a fragile little thing with eyes much like Reed's. Deep and dark with faraway mysterious lights. She appeared to be no older than fifteen, though it was difficult to tell with her body so swollen with child.

The men didn't follow, leaving the women on their own.

For several awkward moments both stood in the middle of the gloomy room eyeing each other, then Tressie gestured toward the crude table Reed had fashioned. There a wooden bowl held red and blue plums picked by Reed the evening before. They were small and tart but very tasty. Tressie dreamed of plum pudding like Mama used to make, but they had no flour or sugar. Bitter Leaf shyly accepted one of the ruby red fruits and put it to her lips.

"I don't suppose you can understand me," Tressie told her, "but it sure is nice to have another woman around." She reached toward the girl's bulging belly. "My mama lost her young'un not long ago."

Bitter Leaf nodded without comprehension and chewed on her plum, allowing Tressie to spread an open hand on her stomach.

"Oh, my. It's moving a lot." Tressie shook her head vigorously. "Very healthy, I'd guess." She fanned both hands over the girl's stomach. Precious life penned up in there, and it grew impatient.

The girl reached out for a curly lock of Tressie's auburn hair. Then she cupped her hand and opened it wide, smiling.

Tressie nodded eagerly and admired her guest's hair in the same way. Babbling on, though she knew Bitter Leaf didn't understand, "You've never had a child before, have you? And I'll bet you're frightened half out of your wits. Well, I think maybe we should just see that you stay here until this baby is born. Right here. No use in you going through this with that galoot of a man out there. Little use he'd be, I'll wager."

Bitter Leaf's answering smile lit up her heart-shaped face and she babbled awhile. Tressie responded by giggling like a girl and Bitter Leaf joined in.

Reed came through the doorway about that time. "Well, I see you two gals are getting along okay. Guess what? Dooley has coffee and some flour and sugar. He'll share it with us for a few days' hospitality. Says he could smell that rabbit stew five miles down the trail. They ain't took the time to campfire cook for three days."

"Reed, her baby is due any day. She ought to stay here till after it's born. That savage out there can't birth this baby. He'll just let her do it on her own, and she's only a child herself."

Reed touched fingers to Tressie's upturned face. "If you don't beat anything, girl." Jerking the hand away, he cleared his throat. "I'll talk to Dooley. I'm sure he'll agree. But Tressie, you need to know she'll probably want to do it her own way, and it's best if you let her. You understand?"

Temporarily distracted by his closeness, she nodded, then mumbled, "Least I can do is hold her hand."

Reed moved away from her, filling her with regret.

Ever since her recovery from the sickness, he had been reluctant to come too close. He seldom touched her or talked overlong with her. What had happened she had no idea. If she let herself think too much about his coolness, an unexplained sadness welled up, immediately followed by a stirring of anger. Venting either to such a stubborn man would be useless.

That evening over supper, Dooley told a strange and wondrous tale. It certainly explained the relationship between the mountain man and his devoted Indian companion.

He related how he had found Bitter Leaf in a village, the sole survivor of a cholera outbreak. "Everyone left her for dead, those that could leave, anyway. She was most gravely ill when I came across her. I doctored her until she recovered, and now she follows me. Thinks I'm a god or some such."

Even considering the man's unforgivable manners, Tressie could understand how Bitter Leaf might feel.

Dooley slurped down great mouthfuls of rabbit stew before

continuing. "That was quite a sight, finding her in that lodge. Her people dressed her for death before they left. She had on new moccasins, her legs were wrapped in scarlet cloth, she was covered in buffalo robes all stitched with porcupine quills."

"When was that? I mean, how long the two of you been together?" Reed asked, sopping out the bottom of his bowl with a biscuit.

"More'n a year ago now, I reckon. I performed the marrying ceremony so we ain't living in sin. Man gets mighty lonely wandering through this vast country by hisself. Itching, if you know what I mean. A woman who can put up with such is a treasure indeed. She's a mite puny and dumb as a rock, but young enough and awful purdy, don't you think?"

Tressie watched the girl eat, eyes downcast, and shuddered. How dreadful to think of this man covering that delicate little thing. When she looked away, she caught Reed's gaze holding on her steady.

He took a quick bite of the bread and complimented her on the first baking she'd done for them. She said nothing.

The men began discussing the gold camps and what was going on in the mad rush the country seemed caught up in.

"It's a sad state of affairs out yonder," Dooley declared, waving a great paw toward the door. "Females deserted or left because their man has died, sitting in their wagons weeping. Some holding dead children. Animals starving yoked to the wagon of an entire family of dead folk. Folks throwing their possessions along the side of the trail to lighten their load for the mountain trek, till they get so desperate they have no food or clothing. Some started out with nothing, thinking only of the gold they'd find at the end of the trail. Many knowing nothing about the countryside."

"What's the government doing about it?" Reed asked.

"What do you expect? Nothing, that's what. They could send

out some troops, check out the trails, at least show folks the way and help them that's stranded. But they're for the most part caught up in that bloody war. Hell, even before, during the California rush, wasn't any better and there wasn't even no war then. Government men are a bunch a useless varmints, want to know what I think. They's a few private citizens helping out, though."

"What do you hear of the war?" Reed asked.

"Last word I heard, Lee had defeated the Union Army at Chancellorsville, but it cost him dearly. Old Stonewall Jackson met his maker there. Shot by mistake by his own men, I hear. Ain't heard much since, and I reckon that was early on this year. In May, near as I could find out. Been a bit out of touch."

Reed pursed his lips and said nothing.

"Young feller like you, how'd you miss it?" Dooley asked.

Tressie jerked a quick look at him. He sounded threateningly casual, and whatever answer Reed might have Tressie considered his own business. Besides, she was frightened of the unspoken answer to Dooley's question.

She interrupted before more could come of the inquiry. "Reed, we could use some water before dark so I can clean up the supper things. Would you mind?"

Obviously Reed welcomed the change of subject, and he gave her a grateful glance before he headed out for the spring where they'd been getting their water since settling in the cabin. He didn't ask Dooley to go along.

That night Tressie offered the only bed to Bitter Leaf, and after much discussion, only some of which she understood, it was decided she and Bitter Leaf would share the bed and the men would sleep on the floor.

During the week that followed, Tressie decided the two men had come to some kind of an understanding, for all talk was of the gold camps. No one made further mention of the war raging between the North and the South. Instead, the men hunted together, sometimes remaining out all day. She and Bitter Leaf searched for berries and edible roots and herbs known to the Indian woman. And they talked, using a crude sign language that both devised as they went along.

In awkward sign Bitter Leaf told Tressie that she had two older sisters and a brother who would one day be chief of their band. She had lost her mother in the cholera epidemic that had almost claimed her own life. This brought the two women closer together, for Tressie sorely missed her own mama. They exchanged words for "mother" and "family" and "love," and finally "sister," reverting to calling each other that in an affectionate way.

Nearly every day Dooley fetched his "squaw" and led her off to the woods. Tressie figured out what they were doing after Bitter Leaf returned with blood on her deerskin dress. Tressie wanted to kill the brute, sneak up on him in the middle of the night and bludgeon him to death with that gun he carried so proudly, as if it were an extension of his fearsome body.

She feared appealing to Reed. Such things were, after all, nobody's business. All she could do was comfort Bitter Leaf in her misery. She had grown so large with the child, and carried it so low, she could scarcely rise from the bed during the last days before the birth.

There were good times, too. Reed fashioned them all boots of deerskin and lined them with rabbit fur. Tressie cherished hers and knew come winter they would be invaluable.

The two men decided that as soon as the baby came and could handle traveling, the foursome would head northwest across the mountains toward the gold camps. The men could seek their fortunes while Dooley converted sinners, Tressie could search for her father, and Bitter Leaf would care for the child. It was a wonderful plan, according to the men. Tressie and Bitter Leaf saw no choice but to follow along, at least until they reached civilization.

While they awaited the birth, Reed withdrew totally from Tressie's company. Despite their plans, she feared any day to find him gone, leaving her to the mercy of Dooley's wishes.

In truth, Reed couldn't stand being around the two women. Though he approved wholly of their friendship, watching Bitter Leaf recalled to him thoughts of his own mother. The fact that this lovely young Indian woman soon would bear a child made the memories even more painful. Reed hadn't known how much he missed growing up without a mother until the big trapper and his wife showed up. Dooley Kling could well be his own father.

As for Tressie, every time he looked at her he experienced the sawtoothed ache of knowing he could never have her. And as she recovered from the ravages of cholera she grew more and more beautiful. Her skin glowed with a healthy sheen, her hair grew into curls that caressed her shoulders, her forest-green eyes flashed with life. And when she laughed...oh, dear God, when she laughed, he thought he would die from wanting her.

So he took to roaming the woods long after the day's game was slain and firewood gathered.

The night Bitter Leaf's baby came, Tressie lay awake, torn between her excitement over the coming event and being on the way again in search of Papa. The Indian girl made no sound, simply shyly touched Tressie's arm, then slipped from the bed and squatted on the floor. Tressie followed and fetched the birthing bed, unrolling the cloth near the girl, who rocked back and forth with her arms clasped around both knees. A patch of moonlight flooding through the open door threw a grotesque humped shadow onto the wall.

In a flash of painful memory Tressie recalled Mama's birthing. How she had labored, sweated, and howled her anguish, and finally died in a room empty of her man, bereft of his love. Bitter Leaf would have Tressie's love and support. Tressie knelt beside her and laid a hand on her back.

"There, there, sweet, sweet girl," Tressie crooned. "I'm here." After a while she moistened a cloth in cold water and placed it around Bitter Leaf's neck. The girl made little noise, just occasionally uttering low, guttural sounds that drifted away as if they'd never been.

By dawn, Tressie was tracking the contractions by the pattern of small sounds. Birth was very near the. She built up the glowing fire and put on a pot of water.

The clatter awoke both men. Dooley pulled on his boots and jacket—they all slept clothed in the small cabin—grabbed his long rifle, and was out the door.

The coward.

While Reed tarried to lace up his hide boots, he watched Tressie's preparations nervously. "Will you be okay"—he gestured—"with this?"

"Oh, I've delivered a child, if that's what you mean. It's her that might not be all right. We'll do the best we can. Women die doing this."

He flinched as if struck, and she remembered too late what he'd said about his own mother. "I know. Can I do anything?"

"I'm sorry. You could bring some more water, then just keep Dooley out of here. I don't trust him to do her good." She poked another stick in the fire as Bitter Leaf bore down and grunted in earnest.

Indian women obviously were not used to much preparation, and Bitter Leaf had shown Tressie how she planned to birth the baby. Surprisingly it wasn't much different than Tressie had witnessed, except she had used scissors to cut the umbilical cord after tying it off, and Bitter Leaf would bite hers in two.

As the girl strained, sweat pouring off her body and muscles bulging, Tressie knelt in front of her and took her hands. She prayed this birth would be luckier than her mother's. Bitter

Leaf pushed and panted and growled her way through each contraction, her face contorting, then going slack.

She squeezed Tressie's hands so tightly the bones made cracking sounds.

Reed returned with the water. She sensed his presence before he spoke. "Is everything okay? Do you need anything?"

"She's almost ready. She just has to do this herself. I can only hang on and let her know I'm here. At least she has that."

'Tressie, girl," Reed said, and cupped a hand on the back of her head.

They stayed that way, watching Bitter Leaf, who never once looked up from her labors. When her water broke, it spread in a dark pool across the pine-board floor.

Too soon the girl tossed back her head, tendons harsh against the sweaty skin, and let out the only cry she had uttered during the entire episode. She reached between her legs to support the head of the child as it emerged.

"Shouldn't she lie down?" Reed asked, watching in awe.

"This is her way." Tressie kept watch as Bitter Leaf cradled the squirming bloody baby.

"Look at that. Dear Lord, look," Reed said. He wanted to cry with the joy of it, like men weren't supposed to do.

"It's a boy. It's a baby boy. You should go now, Reed," Tressie said. She wasn't conscious of his leaving, only that he was no longer there.

Bitter Leaf lifted the child, still attached to her by the wrinkled length of cord, and smiled at Tressie.

Tressie positioned the child across its mother's stomach and tied off the cord in two places with string they'd fashioned from the sinew of one of Dooley's deer kills. Brown eyes swimming in moisture, Bitter Leaf bent to gnaw the cord and separate herself from her baby. Tressie then cleaned out the tiny mouth and blew puffs of air into the red face, just as Bitter Leaf had instructed. The baby gasped and began to cry.

"Well, Dooley, you have yourself a living, breathing son," Tressie said under her breath. But she didn't go call him to look.

An animallike sound from Bitter Leaf caught her attention. The woman's face had gone purple with strain. She should expel the afterbirth easier than that.

The baby in Tressie's arms shivered and squalled, and she focused on him. He needed to be washed and wrapped right now. She was determined he wouldn't die; he just couldn't. The tiny fists flailed the air, spindly legs kicked, and he bawled lustily, bringing a sad grin to Tressie's lips.

"A wonderful sound, little one," she said, and kissed the wrinkled, blood-smeared forehead.

Then she washed the baby with warm water, starting with the thick crop of black hair and ending with the delicate toes. The bath soothed him and he searched her face inquisitively with unfocused eyes. Wrapping him in a portion of the quilt she'd cut up into small squares, Tressie kissed each silken cheek, then held him close to her heart so he could hear the beat. Closing her eyes, she cradled him there for a long while, gently swaying. She wouldn't cry, she just wouldn't. With a sigh she turned to hand him over to his true mother.

The girl lay on the dirt floor curled in a fetal position. Tressie cradled the child in one arm and leaned down to brush long strands of Bitter Leaf's black hair from the sweat-covered face. The brown eyes were open and unseeing. For a moment Tressie thought the girl was dead, but felt then feeble breaths of air from her open mouth.

What was wrong with her?

A brutal contraction hit the girl, drawing her knees even tighter against her chest, and a mass of dark blood spread around her still form. She groaned weakly. Tressie lay the child on the bed and knelt to tend to its mother. Another contraction exposed a tiny head awash in blood.

Tressie cried out. Bitter Leaf was having another child. She'd been carrying twins.

But it wasn't to be. The frail girl bled to death while struggling to birth the second child. Almost before Tressie realized what was happening, Bitter Leaf simply quit breathing. Tressie sat on the floor beside her, holding her hand while tears coursed down her cheeks. So much death everywhere. Would it never end?

She could hear the baby sucking at his fist on the bed, so she roused and went to check on him. From there she could see out the door. Dooley and Reed sat in the sun, backs up against a huge boulder out on the rim of the bluff.

An insane need to punish someone for what had happened washed over her. She raced to the men. Reed struggled to his feet, but Dooley was past being able to rise. Both had been drinking.

'Tressie?' Reed swayed a little, holding himself upright.

She ignored him, preferring Dooley as a target. The attack began fairly controlled, but grew quickly into a mayhem she couldn't control.

"I won't ask where you got that." She indicated the jug Dooley held between his legs. Then, so fast he had no idea it was coming, she kicked out, catching him just above one kneecap. Before he could let out his enraged bellow, she grabbed the whiskey jug and flung it off the side of the mountain.

"While you sat out here getting drunk, your wife was in there dying. And it took her a long time to do it. You monster, you no-account animal."

The tone of her voice rose with each word until she was screaming incoherently. She barely knew what she said, and certainly doubted that he understood any of the accusations. How could a man of his so-called convictions sit out here drinking while his wife bled to death? All men were alike, and women were meant to suffer because of it. She would never forgive Dooley. Him or Papa. Was Reed any better?

"Damn you all, damn you!"

At that moment she longed to punish Papa every bit as much as she did this uncivilized animal of a man. Frustrated at her inability to further put into words how she felt, she fled, ignoring Reed's bewildered expression of sorrow.

She spoke to neither man when later that evening they buried Bitter Leaf and the darkly still baby. Anger left Tressie exhausted, and she preferred to mourn in private, with only God and Bitter Leaf's surviving son as her witness.

Seven

Before daylight Dooley rose and crept in silence to the saddlebags belonging to the breed. The breed put great stock in what he carried; there must be something of great value there, and there was no use in leaving it behind. Very quietly he carried the leather saddlebags outside. It was time to leave.

Before retiring, he had readied everything he would take, secreting the hoard in the woods where he also tied Bitter Leaf's pony. His Enfield rifle stood outside the door, and he eased to it, stepping carefully in the boots the breed had made. Made for quiet walking, they were. He stifled an insane desire to laugh.

No moon shone and it took a while for him to make his way down the steep path and into the stand of pine. He tossed the bags on his horse, mounted up, and rode off, heading high up into the mountains.

As if someone had shaken her, Tressie awoke abruptly. Predawn light touched the windows of the cabin, and she gazed down into the peaceful countenance of Bitter Leaf's beautiful son.

Her mind was boggled by their predicament. There was no milk for him, and she had no idea how far it was to civilization. A trading post or farm would do, but either of those could be a day's walk or more.

She brushed at the tiny fist with the tip of a finger.

"Caleb," she whispered. "Caleb Reed Kling." Much as she hated to add the distasteful surname, Dooley Kling was the child's father. And a boy should carry his father's name.

Before Caleb could set up a howl, she rose from the bed and prepared him a cloth soaked in sugar water. The rosebud mouth sucked noisily at the sugar teat, eyes closed and fists clenched.

Tressie sat on the edge of the bed. The men hadn't returned until after she had gone to bed.

Except for the soft sounds of Caleb's suckling, the cabin was unusually quiet. Kling usually snored up a storm, and Reed wasn't the quietist man sleeping, either. They must be up and about already.

A distant bird song floated in the morning air, and she caught her breath at the beauty of it. Nature certainly wasted no time mourning the loss of one of its precious own. And perhaps that was the way it should be.

"Caleb," she whispered. "Sweet Caleb. I'll take care of you, baby. Don't you worry, you poor little fella. Not a way to start life, without a mama. But never you mind, I'll be your mama."

Reed stood in the middle of the clearing, not wanting to believe what his eyes told him. The Indian pony was gone, as were all of Kling's belongings. The man had lit out, leaving them with the little fellow and no way to ride out for help.

The bastard!

He knuckled bleary eyes and paced around, hoping to find signs of the man. Signs that he was wrong and the trapper had simply ridden out to hunt or set traps. But everything was gone. Things the man wouldn't have taken on such a trip. Dear God, what would they do now? Kling was just like Reed's father and Tressie's, too. Run away and desert his own flesh and blood as if he weren't worth even a thought. Reed stood for a moment on the rim of the trail, staring out across the rugged mountain peaks. Sometimes even the toughest man felt like turning loose and bawling. Instead he trudged silently to the cabin to break the news to Tressie.

For a moment he hesitated in the doorway, gazing in awe. What a beautiful sight they were, this mother crooning to her babe. Tears stung at his eyelids. At times like this his hunger for her overpowered his better sense. They'd take the child and go away together. Anywhere she wanted. He would care for them both and love them. See that the tiny mite never had a day's regret about being unwanted by his callous father. He and Tressie could have other children together. Fear nudged at his heart, making it ache. Women were so fragile, and yet were forced to perform the hardest of all tasks in the world. Bearing children, these lovely beings endured a pain greater than any he could imagine. He hungered to go to her, gather them both in his arms and protect them forever.

Before he could make a move, she sensed him standing there and glanced in his direction. He walked silent as no breeze at all to her side, and when she could see his face she noticed a glint of moisture in the dark eyes.

"How is he?"

"Oh, he's fine. No thanks to his daddy."

Tressie, I'm sorry about the girl...and all." He shrugged and gestured to the outdoors, wondering again how to tell her of their plight.

"I know. Where is he? I'm not giving him this baby, you know. He can't have him. He's not—"

Reed took a deep breath and plunged. "He's gone. Left out, slick as a skinning. You don't have to worry about him wanting that little tyke."

"Oh," she said softly, and glanced down at Caleb, whose wide eyes studied her solemnly. She still didn't realize the gravity of their situation, and Reed wasn't quite ready to tell her.

He took a step closer and peered at the child nested in her arms. The baby gazed up at him with wide dark eyes. "Not so ugly this morning, is he?"

"Why, Reed Bannon, no baby is ugly." Squeezing her eyes tightly shut, she whispered, "There's no milk. What are we going to do? I couldn't stand it if he dies."

He didn't reply and she looked up to see him watching her with such an intent and tender expression that her mind flew back to the time she nursed him back to health. How he lay so helpless and hurt, depending on her. That tie tugged at her heart. He was hers, too, saved for what? To now save this child?

"Oh, God." He dropped to his knees, touched her cheek with the back of one hand. "I wish I could have taken better care of you...of his mama. I just didn't know....I mean I knew, but it didn't seem possible it could happen again. Like some kind of punishment. Dying just like my own mama. I was so sure that this time everything would be all right. That all I needed to do was keep Dooley out of the way. And I..." he leaned his head on her breasts beside the baby. He couldn't tell her the whole truth. How relieved he'd been when she'd made him leave; how he couldn't wait to run away like the coward he was. Just the same as he always did when things got to be too much.

She shifted and embraced him. "What are we going to do now? That's what's important. We can't let Caleb suffer."

"Caleb?"

She nodded her head. "Caleb Reed, I thought. After my grandfather and...well. If that man doesn't want him, he'll not carry his name. We can call him Cale if you like. It has a nice sturdy ring to it."

He noisily cleared his throat. What was he thinking of? She sounded like they were going to take the baby somewhere together and raise him, a half-breed child. *Just like himself* echoed in his mind but he tossed it into the darkness of his spirit. He jerked his hand away and climbed to his feet.

"I'll find him some milk...somewhere. A cow, a goat... surely there's people out there. I'd be best if you stay here with him, and I go."

Her heart swelled into her throat and pounded there fit to choke her. What if he didn't come back? "Why can't we just go to Fort Laramie?"

Reed crossed the small room to sort through the remainder of the supplies. There was hardly anything left. It was a wonder the man hadn't taken it all, but perhaps he was afraid of getting caught if he prowled around inside the cabin. A little flour, sugar, and meal, a double handful of beans, and a water pouch. Hell, the bastard had even taken Reed's saddlebags. He grabbed the water bag and glanced up to see her watching him, waiting for a reply to her question.

"Oh, no, we can't walk all that way. It's at least two days by horseback to the fort. Once down off this mountain there's still the hot windy flatlands to cross. No, you'll be safer here."

She didn't like the idea one bit, but knew he was right. Caleb needed strength before he could safely make that kind of trip. For a long moment she studied Reed's searching eyes, which met hers without flinching. Did she trust him? What choice did she have? She shrugged imperceptibly and fingered her handkerchief pouch from under the mattress. "You'll need this."

He took it. "What's this?"

'To buy the milk,' she said softly.

"Where did this come from?"

"What difference does it make?" she asked. "Just use it."

He took the hanky, then busied himself tying the rawhide strands of the water bag to his belt. There were more important things to consider than why she had kept a few lousy coins a secret from him. He was guilty of hiding things himself, letting her believe they could actually save this newborn child. How could he tell her how slim the chance was of him finding milk or getting back in time? No, it was better if they each carried their own secrets.

She never knew what to make of this man. First he was tender, then distant. He had run before and could do the same again, but surely he wouldn't let this baby starve. Caleb fussed at the sugar teat. How much longer would it keep him satisfied?

Reed crossed to the door, careful not to get too close to the woman and child. He was afraid of what he might do should she reach out.

At the door he spoke without looking back. "I'll be as quick as I can. I'm leaving the rifle, over there in the corner. It's loaded," and he was gone.

For a long while she stared at the empty doorway, until the sound of his going faded. Birds trilled in the warming morning. Caleb had fallen asleep in her arms and she lay him in the middle of the bed.

Then, without conscious thought, she dropped to her knees and rested her forehead on the mattress. She wanted to pray, but all she could think of was, "Dear God, dear God," and she repeated the words over and over with a longing in her soul such as she'd never felt before. *Don't let this child die, too. Please don't.*

She rested there until her knees protested the hard floor. How long should she wait before deciding he wasn't coming back? She had no way of keeping track of the time that passed. And what should she do when she finally knew he wouldn't return? Little Caleb slept on, but too soon he would awaken, and this time he would be hungrier. The sugar teat might not satisfy him, and even if it did, how long would it take a newborn baby to starve to death without milk?

Tressie stepped outside to gaze into the western sky, riffled with clouds that looked like clabbered milk.

As soon as Reed was out of sight of the cabin, he struck out for the river routes. There would be traders along that way. If he had avoided settlements on their trip in, he could no longer do that and save the child. Only a crazy man would think he could accidentally run across a stray cow or goat just waiting to be milked. By midday he cut a well-marked trail. Indians or white man traveled this way on a regular basis. And maybe even soldiers, though Kling had said they were off fighting the war. It was a big country, and the chances of him running across someone who knew him from his days with Quantrill, or later at Pea Ridge, or even the incident with the Union soldier, were nil. He couldn't help being nervous about it, though.

Late evening, and at first he didn't recognize the trading

post, nothing more than a log cabin with no windows and a lean-to where several horses were tied. He eyed a stout Indian pony wearing a saddle with a blanket tossed over it. Two long-legged duns and a red mare were also tied at the rail. In front of the post was a wagon and as he stepped up onto the plank porch, a man came out carrying a sack of feed over one shoulder. He loaded it in the wagon as Reed stepped inside the dark post.

The Indian who obviously owned the pony outside squatted just inside the door. Two men visited with the storekeep, who stood behind a plank counter doling out his wares. It was too dark in the room to make out features, and he was glad of that. He glanced around at the shelves of goods. A wooden barrel in one corner held dry beans. There was a smell of feed and leather in the suffocating air.

The men at the counter, who had suspended their visiting when he entered, went back to their jabbering. Weather and hunting and talk of women.

Then his ears perked.

"Hear there's a new commander down to the fort," one man said.

The storekeeper, who had a nasal twang, replied, "Yep, heard the same. He come up from Missouri with a passel of soldiers. Gonna quieten down the Indians. It got to where the stages and freight wagons couldn't even get through. Savages killed a bunch a whites a time back. That all for you?"

The customer nodded, hefted his purchases and left.

Reed waited his turn, wondering who the Union soldier sent to quell the Indian uprisings could possibly be. Funny they'd take him out of the war, but then after Pea Ridge, there wasn't much war to fight. He figured it was just a matter of time now before Lee surrendered, if he hadn't already.

"Help you?" the storekeep said, and he realized the man was talking to him.

"Milk."

"In tins?"

"Whatever you've got."

"Only have three. Supplies overdue now."

"How about a bottle? You got a baby bottle?"

"Not much call for them." The man eyed Reed.

He nodded. "Still, you got one?"

"Easier if you was to ask for a wet nurse, mister." The man snorted and Reed realized it was meant for a laugh.

Reed drew out the handkerchief and began to untie the knot. "We'll make do, I reckon. How much?"

"Would a whiskey bottle do?"

"Not without one of those...whatchamacallits... uh—a rubber nipple?"

"Well, I sure as toot don't have one of them." The man snorted out another laugh. He took the coins Reed offered, gave him a few in change.

Reed studied his hand a moment, thinking about the sugar teat. "Ill take that whiskey bottle after all," he said. "and a pound of cornmeal...and some beans."

While the man rummaged around under the counter Reed asked, "You know that commander's name, the one who come to Fort Laramie?"

"Nope, never heard it. White-headed, they say. A mite too old to fight in a war, maybe. Good place to dump him. Fort Laramie." He held out a flat-sided empty clear glass bottle. "This do? I'll get'cha the cornmeal and beans."

"Owe you anything for the bottle?"

The man studied him a moment. "Nah, it's okay."

When he left with his meager purchase, the Indian still squatted beside the door. He could have been made of wood. It was all Reed could do to walk past the fine pony without just jumping on its back and riding off hell-bent for leather. But if he did, it would have to be for high country, leaving Tressie to her own devices. She had enough troubles without him leading a bunch of wild Indians right to her door. So he expelled a deep sigh and headed back the way he had come, on foot. He couldn't help but wonder how long three tins of milk would last.

Tressie had grown used to being hungry on the trail, and so didn't notice that she hadn't eaten anything at all that day until late in the afternoon. By then her stomach ached with a need to be fed. She dared not leave Caleb to hunt; just her brief forays into the woods to relieve herself had made her nervous. Suppose he woke and started to cry and choked, or somehow managed to fall off the bed? She knew such thoughts were probably very irrational, but couldn't help it.

The stew pot had been scraped clean the day before, ever since she'd been too distracted to do much about it. Building up the fire, she added a bit of water to the remaining cornmeal and made a couple of johnnycakes.

She ate them standing in the doorway, straining her eyes to catch a first sight of Reed returning. Caleb woke and she changed him, rinsing the soaked cloth and hanging it near the fire to dry.

He began to cry when sucking on both fists brought no results, and Tressie soaked the sugar teat in the last of the sweet water, mopping up every last drop before offering it to the screaming, red-faced baby.

She held him close, sitting outside the cabin on a boulder so she could see Reed as soon as he came up the trail. Caleb was satisfied for a while, then began to whimper and spat out the rag. He turned his head into Tressie's breasts, tiny mouth opened and searching. The incredible mop of black hair tickled at her arm, and his lips made wet spots on the bodice of her dress.

She could hardly stand it when he cried, especially when she couldn't get him to hush.

Standing, she rocked him gently and walked back and forth in front of the cabin, tears streaming down her cheeks. "Hush, darling. Don't cry so. He'll be back. He'll be back real soon."

His little fingers kneaded at her useless breasts.

Suppose Reed didn't return, or found no milk?

"Oh, God, oh, God." Her prayer seemed useless as the burning sun slid behind the mountains to the west and left her and Caleb alone in the frightening dusk. The baby finally cried himself into a restless sleep in her arms, but she continued to hold him.

The grizzly showed up just at full dark, making all the noise in the world circling the cabin.

Snorting, snuffling, his great claws slashed at the sides of the cabin. Tressie cast one frantic glance at the open doorway, over which only a skin hung. Some bears, she knew, weren't actually dangerous to humans. But others, like the giant grizzly, could slice a man in two with one swipe of its vicious paw, and often did.

Heart leaping into her throat, Tressie quickly wrapped Caleb and hid him in the far corner away from the door. Then she hefted the rifle and prepared it to fire. Even the powerful .50-caliber ball might not stop a grizzly, and she would have to reload and fire again before he could cross the room.

Of course, she could hit him between the eyes and maybe

stop him. Tressie positioned herself between Caleb and the doorway, rifle butt snugged into her shoulder.

Outside, the bear grunted and knocked over something, then moved along the side of the cabin, coming closer to the door. Tressie patted the possible bag to check its location. She could scarcely breathe as she listened to the animal. There was no light inside the cabin, and so she could make out starshine through the window and around the skin hanging over the doorway. As he entered, the bear would make a perfect target.

The rifle grew heavy and the barrel began to waver. The muscles in her arms protested keeping the thing aimed. The bear stopped moving. His breath evened out, as if he, too, were listening for danger. Tressie held her own breath. What was he doing?

Caleb hiccuped and Tressie jerked, her attention temporarily caught by the child at her back.

At that precise moment, when she was halfway between seeing to the baby and listening to the bear, the creature let out a wall-shaking roar and burst through the flimsy skin. On hind legs he stood taller than the doorframe, and the heat of his enormous body washed over her. His breath smelled fetid and he stank of his own waste. The tiny room filled with the taste and smell of fear and death. Caleb began to scream bloody murder, and for just an instant Tressie thought about joining him.

She bit at her lip…hard, tasting salt and blood, aimed the rifle, and squeezed the trigger.

The hammer fell and nothing happened! Just that terrible snap that warns of a misfire.

The bear dropped to all fours and snuffled loudly, big head swaying back and forth as he surveyed this strange cave. She couldn't see his face—it was too dark—but she could make out a shape, and its enormity horrified her.

Without taking her eyes away from the looming shadow, she fumbled inside the possible bag, found another cap, and replaced the useless one. All by feel. She wanted to shout at Caleb to shut up so she could think, but his endless crying gave impetus to her need to do this thing right this time.

The animal obviously didn't see well, but he had to smell them, had to be making up his mind whether to eat them for his dinner or just rip them to shreds.

Tressie raised the rifle once again, curved her quivering finger over the trigger, and pulled. She couldn't help shutting her eyes when the thing went off. *Ka-blatt-boom-boom-boom.* The noise ricocheted around the walls of the small room. The bear bellowed and rose once again to his full height so that his head was up in the rafters. Tressie screamed and Caleb, who hadn't stopped screaming, got all the louder.

Reed, who had come up the trail to the cabin just in time to hear the gun discharge, added his own shouts to the cacophony. The bear knocked him aside as it crashed out the door. He climbed to his feet in time to see the staggering, lunging body go over the edge of the cliff, its roar of pain following it into the deep canyon.

It was suddenly so dreadfully still inside the cabin that Reed just knew the wild creature had slain both Tressie and the baby. He hadn't really seen enough to know if perhaps the animal might have carried one of them off the cliff with him.

The stench of blood and black powder permeated the suffocating room. Reed crept through the doorway, feeling a gory dampness brush along the side of his face. The shredded hide dripped gore from the wounded bear.

Despite the ghastly odor and the dreadful stillness, he sensed a living woman and child, as if he could hear them breathing or smell their particular odor. Then he realized why. Tressie was crooning very softly and the child's breath hitched as he cooed back to her.

They were alive!

He fumbled around and found a stub of candle. Brushing away the gray coals in the fireplace, he uncovered a glowing ember, lit a sliver of wood, and touched it to the wick. The golden glow sprung into all corners, revealing utter chaos. And in its midst the woman hunkered in the corner on her heels, rocking the baby. Singing, for chrissakes. She was singing!

❀

Tressie was not aware of his presence until he lit the candle. Even then she continued to soothe Caleb, who had cried so hard she thought he would convulse. She finally had him quieted, mostly because he was too exhausted to cry anymore.

Reed was back and they were safe. At least for the moment. She didn't realize how really terrified she was until Reed gently took the child from her arms. Then she began to shake. She shook so hard she couldn't talk. She couldn't rise from her crouching position, even though it had grown uncomfortable. She could do nothing but huddle there and tremble. When he tried to solace her, she shook her head and shoved him away.

"The-the bab-baby. Feed him. Oh-oh-oh-kay?"

He nodded.

She hadn't asked him if he brought milk, but just to feed the baby. He built up the fire and put on a pot of water to boil. He supposed the milk should be boiled, too, he didn't know. But it was in a tin. It should be safe. And the hot water would warm it. While the water came to a boil, he busied himself figuring out how to stuff a rag in the top of the bottle so that milk could be sucked through it. It would be messy, and not the best, but the child would get some. Failing that, they could always spoon-feed him.

Tressie was finally able to crawl out of the corner and struggle to her feet, but found her hands wouldn't stop shaking long enough to help him. So she sat on the bed, arms wrapped around her shoulders, and watched him. He poured some of the boiling water in the bottle, swished it around and dumped it on the floor, then washed the hunting knife and pried open the tin. With an unsteady hand he poured some in the bottle and added warm water. Not much, for the child's first feeding would have to be small. She approved of his motions. Once he looked at her and smiled and she was able to return the favor, if a bit shakily. He had come back after all. Her prayers had been answered.

Some adjustments made the cloth nipple workable after a fashion, and Caleb concentrated so hard on sucking that the furrowed expression on his little face amused both Reed and Tressie. It took the two of them to get half the feeding in him, burp him, and then get him to finish it off. He spit up some, but seemed to take well to the strange-tasting canned milk.

To her it smelled awful.

She lay him on the bed, put the dry makeshift diaper on in place of the soiled one he wore, then nearly collapsed beside him.

Reed sat on the floor beside the bed. "Well, I see you had a full day."

"Not too bad. How was yours?" she murmured, and grabbed his big hand in hers.

Holding it to her lips, she remained that way for a while.

Then he reached up and touched her cheek with the other hand. She relaxed, and the next thing she knew it was morning. Caleb was gone from his place beside her and the cabin was empty.

She stretched full length, making her muscles and bones pop and crack. They were sore and she felt in bad need of a bath. The stench in the cabin was overpowering. She'd never get it out of there.

Barefoot, she went outside into another sunny day. Did it never rain in this country? She didn't see Reed and Caleb anywhere, but after watching him with the baby last night, she didn't worry. He was probably teaching the boy how to cut trail, or maybe how to suck juice out of a cactus. Whatever, she had only one thing on her mind.

The spring near the cabin didn't have a bowl deep enough to bathe in, but she could certainly wash off. Stripping out of her dress, she knelt in the cool wet moss of the bank and began to splash icy cold water over her body, beginning with her face and rubbing down over her breasts, flat stomach, and thighs.

Reed came upon her as she stood to finish washing. Caleb slept in his arms, and he nested the baby safely on his quilt in the crunchy dried leaves nearby. He walked up behind her, eyes drinking in the delicate curve of backbone, the slight flare of slim hips, the long lean look of her exquisite legs.

She threw her head back and ran her fingers between her breasts and down into the pale nest of hair. She shivered with desire at her own touch, and at that moment sensed him behind her. She turned and lifted her hand toward him, fingers uncurling. He stepped forward, their gaze locked, and she eased into his arms.

He massaged the ridges of her backbone down into the cleft of her hips, while the other hand spread in her thick auburn hair. Their lips met, tasted, hesitated, then drank deeply.

She fumbled with the buttons of his shirt, pressing rigid nipples against his broad chest as she pulled away the fabric. Then the belt buckle, the buttons of the fly, freeing his manhood with one swift motion, then taking him in her fist. He was suffused in warmth, huge and tender, and her need tasted sweet and bright as the day.

He moaned against the thrust of her tongue in the warm recesses of his mouth. Lifting her effortlessly, he lay her on the cool moss, kneeling astride her.

Nearby the baby sucked at his fist, smacking loudly.

Tressie smiled and met Reed's eager lips.

"I love you," he told her between hot kisses, saying it into her flesh with a passion that surprised her.

His long black hair fell over her face when he lowered himself to embrace every inch of her body, covering her with his need and his heat and his aroma. When he slipped inside her, she raised her hips to meet him and hung on. His lips ravished every inch of her—the pulse in her throat, the rosy tips of each breast, the satiny stomach—and she felt a quivering deep inside like a great starving beast rousing from a long slumber.

Still he held her tightly and tasted of her, making her wait for that final ride that would end all too soon. He rocked backward, pulling her into a sitting position beneath him, and she thought she would explode with the feel of him filling the core of her being. His manhood throbbed inside her, exploring where no one but he had ever been. At last he rocked her backward, cradled her head on his arms, and brought her to climax, joining her with a shout that woke the baby.

He rolled to her side, laughing. Slick with the mixture of their perspiration, she panted and coiled backward into his arms to rest, him soft and satisfied against her backbone.

He said the words again. "I love you, Tressie, I love you."

She didn't know what to make of that. All she could think of at that moment was that she was not supposed to let herself love a man so like her traitorous father.

But he had returned. Not like her father at all.

Yet, no matter how she felt in his arms, no matter the bliss, her mind kept coming back to Papa's treachery. How could she dare trust a man so like him? How could she believe his declaration of love and return it when he might only be waiting for the right time to walk away and not even look back? He would wait until she was helpless, most vulnerable, then leave her.

He hadn't left her when she was so ill, and he had returned with milk for the baby, yet she couldn't drive the insidious fear from her mind that he would leave her when she grew to trust him the most…just like Papa.

But oh, Lord, did this man make her feel wonderful.

Eight

Reed fashioned a small pack, mostly things for the baby. He would carry everything else. There wasn't time to bemoan the theft of the saddlebags; he couldn't remember what had been in them.

He and Tressie had slept together, Caleb between them. Like a real family. He waited until dawn to awaken her, for she had risen twice in the night to feed the baby. They'd cooked the beans overnight and had them for breakfast along with corn pone. The meal would have to do them a while.

Once everything was ready, he lifted her hair to settle the pack on her back

"Good thing there's not much left in the way of supplies. Makes less to carry. We'll take turns with the baby, if you like. I kind of enjoy toting the little tyke. He has such a damn-you quizzical look on that monkey face."

"I'm worried about him making the trip," she said quietly.

Without answering, he tested the pack, fingers lingering on the warm skin of her upper arm. "We don't have a choice. The milk will last only another day or so. We can stop at the post first, see if their supplies came. If not, there are other posts along the river. Once we get to Fort Laramie, we'll be okay. There are Army doctors and women there. A sutler's store, too. And a stage line."

The old fear returned. When they reached civilization, he would dump her the first place she'd be safe and take off. Just because he told her he loved her in the heat of passion, once she came to her senses she didn't believe him.

He noticed her silence. "What's wrong?"

"Nothing, I guess. I…what are we going to do? At Fort Laramie, I mean?"

"What do you want to do, girl? From there you can head west and find your father. That is what you want, isn't it?"

"Of course, but I thought maybe we could forget all that. Go someplace together, where we could maybe—?"

"Maybe what? Settle down? Sorry. I've got other things to do. I'm sorry about…I mean, yesterday, I didn't mean to let that get out of hand." Perhaps his reply came out more harsh than he had intended, but he wouldn't take it back now. He turned away. God, if only they could. He had other places to be, things to prove to himself. And she must finish her own quest.

"I know." She was utterly miserable. Damn him for apologizing, for making her feel like a woman scorned. Yet, hadn't she known this all along? Why should she be surprised?

He studied her a moment, then circled around and put the tip of a finger under her chin, tilting upward so that she had to look at him. "You don't want me, not really. We both know why, don't we?" Silently he thought, one coward is quite enough for any woman.

She nodded and didn't say anything. He had told her he loved her, but it didn't mean he did.

It had just been something to say. Otherwise he'd try to talk her into staying with him, for his own selfish needs. Again, she'd made a fool of herself where this man was concerned. But she wasn't sorry they had made love. She cherished the memory like she cherished those memories of home that kept her going when things were tough. No matter where she went or what she did, she would never forget the way this man had made her feel when he took her body to his. When he had put his lips on hers, when he touched her and gazed at her with those bottomless eyes. He couldn't make that feeling go away by leaving her somewhere.

"Well," she said too brightly, "if you're ready, let's get going to Fort Laramie."

Caleb proved to be a tough little traveler. Though the tinned milk caused his stomach some trouble, he was soon over that and bobbed along in a pouchlike sling strapped either to Tressie's bosom or Reed's chest.

The trip took the better part of four days. Of a morning he would boil enough water to last until they camped for the night. The heat of the sun kept the water warm enough for the baby when mixed with the milk. They lost some milk because Caleb couldn't drink an entire can before it soured in the dreadful heat. Replacement proved not to be a problem. She was surprised at the trading posts in the otherwise barren country. It seemed trappers, miners, travelers, and even Indians were numerous enough to support such merchants. Her stash of coins dwindled, though, for things were expensive. She despaired of having enough to board the stage when they reached Fort Laramie.

Late afternoon of the fourth day Reed pointed out their destination. It was a disappointment to her, that gathering of scattered buildings resting on a knoll that somewhat resembled a giant egg sliced in half. Thus situated on the wide plain, Fort Laramie squatted in the crooks of the Laramie and the North Platte rivers.

The icy cold, clear water, snowmelt from high in the mountains, curled around the western flank of the numerous plank and adobe buildings. Tressie hadn't expected the fort to be so large, with so many structures spread like boulders after an avalanche. The fort had no walls. Reed told her they had been torn down years before, not long after the Army took over the trading post from the American Fur Company.

"Hell, Indians ride right in among them now. It's become the laughingstock of this country, this fort that isn't a fort. Said by some to be totally indefensible."

Her eyes grew wide at the tale. "But aren't there soldiers there? Won't we be safe from Indians?"

He only chuckled. He didn't expect them to be safe from Indians anywhere they went from now on, but he didn't tell her that. Oddly, that thought reminded him of the deerskin pouch he'd carried since leaving his mother's people many years earlier. And he remembered then that it had been in the saddlebags Kling had stolen. It had belonged, not to his mother but to his father, a keepsake of sorts that his grandmother assumed he might want. Reed wondered why he had kept it around so long, and felt a surprising relief that it was gone. He'd never been able to simply throw the thing away.

From the very moment they caught sight of Fort Laramie, she'd hated it. Persistent dust, kicked up by heavy wagon and horse traffic, billowed into the endless wind. Crowds of ruffians milled about on foot as if they had no destination. She was, however, reassured by the sign of a few soldiers apparently on guard duty. There were also Indians and fur-clothed mountain men, traders and freighters, barking dogs and stomping horses, all making more noise than she'd ever heard in her entire life. Then there was the stench. Thank God for prairie winds.

Reed had suggested that she wear a dress so she would be decently covered, and to her mind that simply made matters worse. Every man turned to stare and comment as she followed him between the buildings. She saw few women. They were, he explained, officers' wives and they lived in the married men's quarters.

He left her and Caleb in the sutler's store, where she spent one of her coins for a few cans of milk and, wonder of wonders, an actual bottle complete with rubber nipple. The kindly storekeeper found her a place to rest in the back room, and Reed set out to do his business.

Just the proximity of the men in blue uniforms made him extremely edgy. No doubt his description could be found on wanted posters in the States, but he hoped that with the war and the gold rush, the territories were being ignored when it came to law enforcement. It didn't matter, though, for the sooner he could get away from all these boys in blue, the better he would feel. Would he ever be free, or was he destined to run and hide the rest of his life for a series of very dumb mistakes? Maybe eventually Quantrill's riders would forget the man who deserted them at the battle of Lexington, and the Rebs, too, but he doubted that the Union Army would soon forget that he was a horse thief. He hoped to God he wasn't also a killer.

Spotting the Indian tepees on the outskirts of the fort, he decided that there he might find answers to some of his questions without risking his freedom.

The Indians were Oglala Sioux, mostly women and children, with a few less savory braves hanging around. They had set up a regular village upstream a ways from the fort and welcomed him because he spoke their language. He looked like one of them even if he did sound like a white man.

A young boy, no older than twelve or so, fell in with Reed as he entered what the soldiers called "Squaw Town."

After the polite amenities were out of the way, Reed asked the boy, "Who commands the fort?"

"You are from the People?" the boy asked, sniggering behind a hand at Reed's accent.

"My mother was. Tell me about this place."

"They are here to kill the People. They say not, that they are friendly. Their Colonel Collins lies well." The boy grinned up at Reed. "But so do we, when it comes to the whites."

"This Colonel Collins, when did he come here? Where is he from?"

"They say he came from the white man's war, a place called Missouri, to make peace with us." The boy laughed like the sharp bark of a dog. "I wish I was old enough to fight them. Soon, though."

Reed shuddered at the expression of malice on the youngster's face. He could hardly blame the boy, yet he would one day die because of it. There was very little Reed could do about it.

Very little anyone could do, really. The end of this great nation was coming as surely as the wind swept the plains. Once the Yanks licked the Rebs, they'd spit in their hands and head west, and they wouldn't stop until they'd cleared the territories of every Indian who wouldn't surrender. He wanted to tell the boy to put on white man's clothes and go on with his life away from all this, but he didn't. That was no answer. Reed knew that all too well. Sooner or later, you had to pay your dues.

Squaw Town was aptly named, for the only men there were small boys and very old men. From the boy's mother and sister, who worked for the soldiers washing and mending clothes and cleaning the barracks, Reed learned that the braves were elsewhere. This appeared to be an open secret, but one which they would not discuss in great detail. Perhaps the Sioux also realized their own fate and were getting ready for the last battles, gathering with other tribes to bring down on the white man the wrath of their spirit Gods. It would be a great and wondrous battle, and Reed wondered if he might not join them. Surely a way to earn his own warrior feathers.

At last he headed back to the fort. At the sutler's he found Tressie sound asleep on a pallet in the back room of the store, Caleb nestled in the crook of her arm. He struck a deal with the sutler, trading the Kentucky rifle for more tins of milk and enough cash to buy a stagecoach ticket to Virginia City for her and the baby.

"The Overland's got a hotel where she can put up for the night. Stage won't get in till tomorrow," the storekeeper told him. "You ain't going with the little lady?"

Reed shook his head. "Need a job for a while."

The sutler studied him. "You don't talk like a blamed Indian, but you shore look like one. Don't hire Indians except as scouts. You scout, do you? Track your own kind?"

Reed didn't like the man, despite his kindness to Tressie. He had a streak in him that prodded a man. "Nope. I'll find something. Thanks for your kindness to the girl."

"Think nothing of it. She'll have a hard row to hoe, that one. Having that half-breed kid and all. She might ought to have drowned it, been better off."

Reed ground his teeth and took a step backward to keep from hitting the man. 'Tressie. Tressie, girl. Git on out here," he shouted, not taking his flintlike gaze from the sutler, whose expression seemed to say, *Go ahead and hit me, see what happens.* Reed knew how tough these men had to be, and had no real desire to tangle with this one, who was broad as a bull.

Just as Tressie appeared from the stock room holding Caleb, the front door burst open and two soldiers came in. They paid no attention either to her or to Reed, but continued a conversation that had obviously begun out on the street.

"He is, too, a dirty Reb, I don't care what you say," one told the other. "Quantrill is nothing but a killer. He ain't no soldier, on either side."

"Well, may be, but that just shows you don't know everything. He's a captain in the dang Confederate Army, I know that for a fact."

Reed's fingers tightened on Tressie's elbow and she glanced at him sharply. He seemed not to notice, but was watching the two soldiers with an intensity she found unnerving.

The smaller of the two soldiers, who wore an impressive black mustache, whirled on the one who had just spoken, a tall redneck farm boy, by the look of him. "Then you explain to me why, if he's a soldier, did he attack and murder all those civilians down in Lawrence? Tell me that, smart aleck."

"They was probably hiding bushwhackers or the like."

The short man hawked and spit in the direction of a large brass spittoon near the door. He missed, but paid that no mind. "You jest better get your loyalties straight, Nixon, afore the colonel hears you defending a no-account, back-shooting, baby-killing coward like Quantrill and his four hundred. I get any one of them in my sights and it's so long, you mealy-mouth coward. And I won't wait for him to explain he was just doing his soldierly duty, neither."

The tirade heaped upon the redneck soldier made his lantern-jawed cheeks redden, and he flicked a glance toward Tressie. "'Scuse us, ma'am," he said, touching the brim of his hat with one finger.

Reed, lips drawn so tight there were spots of white around his mouth, ducked his head and turned his back to the two soldiers.

"Hey, you, Indian," the tall one said. 'You hadn't ought to touch that little lady. You two ain't together, are you?"

Obviously the man was looking for a way to extricate himself from the embarrassment heaped upon him by his companion, and decided to pass it on to another victim. Reed was in the way.

Tressie looked up at him, watched with fascination the transformation from fury to docility cross Reed's face. Even the tone of his voice changed. "No, we're not together. I just helped her find her way to the fort."

The soldier touched the butt of a weapon strapped to his waist. "Then you best just move on. You got her here, didn't you? Now, little lady," the man said, and this time removed the hat to reveal a crop of red hair, "if I could be of assistance. You planning on taking the stage?"

Tressie nodded and shot a silent plea toward Reed. He turned and stepped away from her.

"Well, then," the soldier said, and offered his arm. "You just come with me. The Overland's got a hotel, and I'll see you and the little one are settled."

Helplessly, Tressie tucked her hand into the crook of the man's arm and, glancing once again at Reed, went with the soldier out the door and onto the dusty grounds.

"You hadn't ought to be traveling alone, ma'am."

"I—I know, but I—"

The man interrupted, "Where are you headed? California?"

"No. No, I'm meeting my husband in Virginia City," she finally managed.

"Not many women out there except for...well...uh—"

"Yes, well…" Tressie hoped the man would just shut up. She wanted to turn around and look for Reed. Surely he was following her. Why had he acted like that? This man had no right to treat him like some savage. He was more white man than Indian. Couldn't they see that? Of course, his hair had grown so long that it hung down between his shoulder blades.

"How long he been gone?" the soldier asked, and gazed pointedly at Caleb, riding on Tressie's left arm.

"Over a year," she said, then wanted to call the words back immediately, for she realized the blunder. The man could certainly count, even if he might have to use his fingers.

The freckled skin of his face flushed bright red, and the soldier stared straight ahead, taking several more steps without saying anything. Then he stopped, took his arm from her grip, and pointed across the way. "Yonder's the hotel. I'd best get back to my barracks."

Tressie's mouth dropped open at his scathing tone. He muttered something about loose women that would lay with redskins and stomped off, beating dust out of his hat with swift thumps across one thigh.

"You knotheaded, loco, stump-kicking—"

Reed came up behind her and took her elbow. "Whoa, Tressie. That's no way for a loose woman to talk."

'You just let him talk to you like dirt and now you think it's funny he treated me the same?"

"Better get used to it if you're gonna raise Caleb. He got his looks from his mama, and he'll never pass for white, no matter what you do."

'You pass," she insisted with a stubborn set to her lip.

Anger crossed his face. "That's been my mistake, but it does keep a fella from getting his teeth kicked out in some quarters." His eyes flashed at her. "Think I ought to get a haircut?"

Tressie couldn't tell if the sparkle in his eye was mischief or irritation. But she was just put out enough herself to snap at him, no matter which it was. "Why should I care one way or the other? You're leaving us here and going your way."

He chewed on that a moment, all the while steering her toward the Overland Hotel. "True. It's best that way and you know it. It's not like I'm deserting you and Caleb. I just don't see any sense to it. Helping you look for your pa in this big country when he—" Reed clamped his lips.

He might have rescued her, but he remained too stubborn to commit to her and Caleb. *Well, good*, she thought. *Fine. Just fine. I don't need him anyway.* If they hadn't been stepping through the door of the establishment at that very moment, she would have told him that she was tired of needing any man, and at that moment wished them all a good trip right straight off the edge of the earth, cowards that they were. As it was, she held her tongue on that subject, smiled at the clerk, and presented her stage ticket, acting as if Reed were a piece of furniture.

When she started to follow the clerk's directions on finding her room, Reed took her arm. "Wait a minute."

"Why? So you can tell me again how little you care what happens to me? No. You be on your way. Do whatever it is you have to do. Caleb and I will go to Virginia City and we'll do just fine, thank you. As for you and I, we're just about even on favors, so let's leave it at that."

With a feeling of deep loss, he watched her disappear down the dark hallway. Never in his life had he wanted anything so badly as he wanted a life with her and the baby. But he couldn't go with her. He was worthless to any woman, pursued by soldiers from both sides of that thankless war. Tressie would do better on her own. She was young and tough. Who would harm a mother and child?

Such thoughts reminded him of the story he'd heard about Quantrill's raid on Lawrence.

Could it be true? If so, he thanked God he hadn't remained with the four hundred. Was Quantrill a butcher despite his motives? Reed had seen firsthand his devotion to the cause that translated into vicious debauchery at the battle of Lexington. Soon after, Reed left his command to join up with Ben McCulloch and his band of five thousand Indian soldiers.

At the Battle of Pea Ridge all hell broke loose. The survivors of that bloody fight scattered to the winds, no food, no boots, no clothing. Hunting the lines, stragglers from the near massacre of Rebel forces dug turnips and onions from abandoned gardens to survive. Many simply headed for home, calling the war over.

He might have made it back to the front lines of the battling Confederate forces without incident, had it not been for running up against a colonel who remembered him from

Quantrill's forces. Who knew he had deserted that band, and accused him of being a traitor.

Reed had lost his weapon at Pea Ridge, and so he fled the accusations.

Come the following spring, outside St. Louis he stole a horse from a Union Army trader, who shot him in the back. Carrying the bullet in his shoulder, he headed north, but not before he shot a Union cavalry private who was in hot pursuit. Reed took that bullet with him right to Tressie's door. If not for her, he would have died. Should any of Quantrill's men ever find him, they'd kill him. On the other hand, the Union Army would surely hang him for the horse thief he was. Never mind what McCulloch's men would do.

He left the Overland Hotel and didn't look back.

In dire need of a bath, Tressie asked for extra water, and washed both herself and Caleb in a shallow dish beside the lumpy cot provided by the Overland Stage Company. She paid no attention to the sagging mattress, for it felt so good to lie down on a real bed that nothing else mattered. The sun had almost gone down, and she was hungry, but both she and the baby fell asleep after he took some milk.

When Caleb awoke her to be fed, she was surprised to see that it was dark outside. Outside, the call of sentries shouting their "All's well," and an occasional whinny or snort of an animal.

Otherwise, the fort seemed to have settled in for the night. She had no way of knowing what time it was. She changed Caleb, rinsed out his diaper in the scummy wash water from earlier in the evening, draped the diaper over the foot of the bed, and fell back into an exhausted sleep. They were awakened by morning reveille. She couldn't remember the last time she had slept so soundly or so long.

After changing Caleb and feeding him, she took her

handkerchief pouch from her pocket and counted the few coins left there. How was she going to go so far without food? Perhaps the stage line provided food along the way, she didn't know. The idea of the trip across the rugged mountains terrified her. And all the talk she'd heard about Indians being on the rampage. She wished that she and Reed could just walk to Virginia City. They'd done all right on foot so far, hadn't they?

Caleb whimpered and she touched a finger to his chin. "Such a good boy," she cooed. He kicked and waved his arms about. She was sure he recognized her and she hugged him. Her baby, her darling baby boy.

Certainly walking cross-country would be too hard on a newborn, but she was afraid that a baby so young wouldn't even survive the stage trip. They couldn't stay here, though. This filthy, uncivilized Army post had no facilities for a family unless the father was in the military. And then she surmised it would be mighty lean pickings.

"You've gone and got yourself between a rock and a hard place," she scolded aloud.

Caleb watched her with solemn dark eyes. She kissed his velvety soft cheek and he rolled his head to search her face with tongue and lips. He wanted a breast, this child, and she wished she had a full one to give him. That realization led her to thoughts of Reed Bannon's lips at her breast. She flushed hotly and pushed those thoughts away. He was out of their life, and she would have to forget him.

How wrong she was, for when she stepped out into the morning sunshine, there stood Reed grinning at her like nothing had happened at all. Somehow he'd gotten a bath and had his hair cut. It changed him, made him appear more vulnerable.

She swept past him. He caught up, his long legs easily matching her own graceful stride. Scowling, she said, "What do you want?"

'To wave good-bye."

"You could have done that without—without—oh, shoot."

"Slow down, you're jostling him. Look at the little tyke."

Tressie set her chin higher and kept right on marching.

"He's going to—oops, see there," Reed said, just as Caleb upchucked all down the front of her dress.

"Look what you made him do," she said.

He spread one large hand over his own chest and widened his eyes. "Not I, ma'am. Here, let me help." He reached for the baby.

"Go away. Just go away." She slapped at his hand.

He tilted his head and watched her blot at the mess with Caleb's spare diaper. He pointed. "There. A spot right there."

Glaring, Tressie wiped some more. Caleb began to cry.

"Oh, darling, it's okay," she crooned. "Look! Now you've made him cry."

"Don't be mad at me. God, it's such a beautiful morning."

"How can you tell? Look around us. At the filth and noise and stench. How do people live this way?"

He shrugged. "Beats me. Give me the rag. I'll wash it," he said, grabbing the diaper and rinsing it out in a nearby horse trough.

When he came back, holding out the cloth so she could finish her cleanup job, their eyes caught, stumbled, and fell over each other. A flush grew up her neck and onto her cheeks. He grinned, his white teeth flashing like pearls against the golden brown skin. Obviously they were both remembering a hot night on a creek bank, and a shared bath.

"Damn you, Reed Bannon," Tressie said fondly. "Are you always going to be able to do this to me?"

"I hope so, girl. I truly hope so."

"Oh, why didn't you just keep on walking when you left me yesterday? I was good and mad at you and could have ridden out of here without any qualms. Now…"

"Now what, darlin'? It'll work out. I got promise of a job

with a new freight line following the Oregon Trail. I thought about never seeing you and the tyke again, and I just couldn't imagine it. So when I get enough money together I'll come along to Virginia City. I guess I'm just no good at saying good-bye, Tressie. I'll be there. Maybe by then you'll have decided to give up lookin' for your pa." *And half the territory will have given up looking for me.* He drew a breath past the thought and went on. "Anyway, we'll see where we go from there."

"Why are you promising me that? All along you said we wouldn't be together anyway. Now all of a sudden you're telling me that as soon as you can, you'll be there. You're just doing this so you won't feel guilty, so you can be on your way without feeling bad."

"Oh, I'll be there; I just don't know when. We don't have enough money for both of us to ride or I'd go with you, I swear. I thought I could just walk away, but I can't. You and me, well, we'll just have to work something out. I promise I'll get there. It'll just take a while."

"How will you find us? Please don't do this to me, please. I'm scared enough as it is. Don't make a promise you have no intention of keeping."

She had a feeling she knew why men sometimes cussed a blue streak. She so wanted to do just that. He had put her in an impossible situation. She couldn't refuse to take the stage for Caleb's sake, yet if she rode away she had a feeling deep inside that she would never see Reed Bannon again.

'You're deserting me, too. Just like Papa did. No matter what you say." She backed off a step, hating what she was feeling.

"We ain't married, and it's not my fault what your papa did, don't you see that? What I do will be strictly Reed Bannon, not your Pa Evan Majors. I'll join you as soon as I can, but I don't recall ever asking you to marry me or saying we would be together. I won't just desert you. I'll come and make sure you're okay. Then we'll talk some more. That's as best as I can do, Tressie. There are some things you just don't know about, and it's better you don't."

"Oh, you mean like the law is after you? And that's why you wouldn't follow the Oregon Trail and we had to take off through those devilish sand hills. What haven't you told me? Why do you have to keep on running away?"

He studied her closely, and she didn't back down one bit. Caleb sensed the tension and set up his own howl, which they both ignored.

"You know, Dooley hit it square when he said that you're a whole lot of spunky gal. You'll need it, 'cause you're gonna have to be real tough to raise that Indian young'un in a white world. And he'll have it even harder. I know that as good as most."

"Damn you, you could be his father if you weren't such a coward," she spat, and pushed past him carrying the crying child.

She'd called it right that time, and Reed didn't try to follow, but that afternoon he was there when she and Caleb boarded the stage. He kept his lips pressed tightly together and there was a glint in his eyes that turned them to chips of hard rock.

She didn't let him catch her looking his way and spoke not a word, but climbed aboard the high-wheeled coach so that her back was to him. She wondered how long he stood in the dust kicked up by the team before he turned and walked away. The thought brought tears to her eyes, but she wiped them with determined swipes of her fingers.

Nine

The Bozeman Trail, according to the elderly gentleman who sat with Tressie, had only opened that year and already had attracted the attention of the Sioux, Arapaho, and Cheyenne, who earlier were content to concentrate their raids on folks traveling the Platte River Road farther south.

The portly man dressed in black, who introduced himself as Sir Harry Crenshaw, seemed determined to educate her on the history of the territory.

"Fools built this road through their sacred grounds, you know. Then when the savages naturally protested, the Army arrived to look out for us. Now they are astonished to find two routes to guard instead of one. Your colonial government has a sense of humor, but then I suppose it has to, given its propensity toward horrendous errors of judgment."

This Englishman, who because of his accent she concluded actually spoke another language altogether from hers, occupied the choice seat on the stage alongside her. Because of the baby, other passengers had deferred to her and let her sit with royalty just behind the front boot. Riding backward was disconcerting at first, but she and the privileged gentleman were less crowded.

Three passengers on the middle bench bumped knees with the three on the back one.

She was told the stage wasn't filled to capacity, but could not see where another body could be crammed. There were eight inside and four up top. When the driver set the coach in motion, she gritted her teeth and gripped the floor with her toes through the bottoms of her deerskin boots. Despite the lingering heat, she had chosen to wear the knee-high, comfortable footwear under the long skirts of her dress. The incessant rocking and jouncing unsettled her stomach, and she worried about Caleb's digestion over the long trip. After all, they were still traveling on fairly level land. What would come when the stage climbed into those towering mountains, she could only guess.

Caleb spit up a lot, and it was difficult to keep the thick dust away from his eyes, mouth, and nose, yet he seldom complained. As the day grew hotter, the curtains covering the windows were opened to let in grit-thick air. Otherwise everyone would have suffocated.

The stage traveled hell-bent for leather, making her feel as if she had lassoed a cyclone and couldn't let go of the rope. No wonder these marvels of transportation could reach the West Coast in less than twenty days. The wheels scarcely touched the ground except when the contraption clattered to a halt. The only breaks allowed the suffering passengers were the four-minute stops to change horses. Other than that, passengers were allowed two rest stops in a twenty-four-hour period. When she learned this, she looked forward eagerly to the first stop, where she and the baby could rest and wash up. She soon found out how far from luxurious those stops were.

The last to climb wearily from the coach, she gratefully took the offered hand of her seat companion and, clutching Caleb, put her feet on each narrow step with great care. The only other woman aboard stood near the home station, splashing her face over a pan of water. She wore a handsome brown linen dress with a matching bonnet, gloves and fine button-up shoes, and carried a small leather satchel.

Sir Harry herded Tressie to the washbasin when the woman moved aside. He appeared to have appointed himself her guardian. After cleaning her face and hands, Tressie attempted to wash some of the dust from Caleb, who kicked and squalled at the touch of the cold rag.

The woman in brown had been watching her closely since disembarking. In her worn muslin dress she felt uncomfortable under the scrutiny. The woman approached when Tressie moved away from the wash pan to make room for the other passengers,

"He's awfully wee for such a trip, isn't he?" she asked.

With a cool nod, Tressie lay Caleb on the log bench set up on one end of the crude building.

Did the woman suppose she had other choices? She unwrapped his clothing and diaper and did the best she could to clean the poor little mite up before fastening on the spare diaper.

"My name is Kate Flanningan," the woman said, and wrinkled her nose through a hurried scrubbing of the dirty diaper in the water left from the passengers' washing. It wasn't until Tressie settled to feed Caleb that the woman began to chatter.

"I'm joining my husband in Virginia City. I've never seen the mountains. I suppose they're enormous. We've lived in St. Louis since we married, but Ezekiel grew tired of running a mercantile. His father owns a freight lines, and they're expanding into the West, so this seemed an ideal time for Zeke and me to make a change. Before we get set in a rut, his father said." The woman laughed nervously, as if wondering at the desires of such men.

"It sounds like an adventure," Tressie said, and propped Caleb over her shoulder to burp. "I'm famished. What do you suppose there'll be to eat?"

"I don't know," Tressie replied, "but it couldn't matter to me.

I'll eat anything that doesn't bite me first." She was glad Kate would rather talk about herself than ask more questions.

When they stepped inside the station, Tressie almost changed her idea of what she would and wouldn't eat. She reluctantly handed over one of her precious coins for a decidedly gray chunk of fried pork fat, mustard greens, a stale biscuit, and a cup of gritty coffee. She and Kate carried the poor fare back outside and ate it in competition with flies and assorted other crawling and flying insects.

Many of the passengers had brought along their own canteens of water. All Tressie had was a supply of boiled water for Caleb's milk. Afraid to drink it and run the baby short, she approached the stationmaster's son, a rangy, bucktoothed boy burned black by the incessant sun. He grudgingly fetched her a tin cup of tepid orange water that tasted brackish and reminded Tressie that she'd once contracted cholera from bad water.

Too soon came the shout, "All aboard. *Awaaaaay!*" and they were once again lurching along the trail.

Once under way, Sir Harry remarked, "During the next rest stop they'll let us lie down for a few hours. Undoubtedly, it'll be a miracle if we aren't all scalped in our sleep."

The remark did little to ease her mind. In the beginning she had worried more about Caleb standing up to the trip than anything else. Now she could add to that visions of hoards of Indian braves riding down on them, shouting and waving knives and hatchets.

"I thought the Army was guarding the route," she said.

"This is the Powder River Run, child. We're for the most part on our way into gold mining country. Speculators and the like. Now who do you think is more important to the stage line and the Army: folks going to California and paying six hundred dollars for the privilege, or us poor misled individuals out seeking our fortune?"

Tressie sighed and leaned her head back to close her burning eyes. She kept Caleb's face shielded with one corner of his quilt. He had been so good. Sometimes he fussed, but mostly he slept. When he made no sounds at all, she worried.

She must have dozed, for when next she looked out the window she beheld the huge purple wall of the Bighorn Mountains. Then the trip got really rough.

Though it was only early September, the higher jagged peaks lay buried under mounds of pristine snow. When the stage wasn't struggling upward along the edge of a precipice, it was skidding almost straight down. It forded swift-flowing creeks and sometimes the passengers had to get out and push until the great wheels rolled free of thigh-deep mud. Tressie and Kate were spared, but not Sir Harry, who didn't seem to mind at all muddying his fancy clothing.

Once, the terrified passengers spent the better part of an afternoon watching a long line of Indian braves ride the ridge above, matching their pace.

As the punishing trip progressed, she vowed to never again deliberately get on board such a horrendous vehicle, not even for one single moment. She continued to vow this over and over as she crawled in or out of the stage, or tasted mustard greens and fried pork fat or rancid corn dodgers. Even walking and sleeping and eating on the ground was preferable to such torture. She found herself longing for the days spent with Reed Bannon on the trail. If it weren't for the constant sightings of Indians, and the nearly impassable, precarious trail, she would have climbed right down from that stage and set out walking, baby and all.

When the stage crossed the Bighorn River, the trail bent west, and Tressie felt that surely they would soon spot Virginia City. Caleb was out of milk, but tethered in the brush near a station stop, miracle of miracles, she spied a milk goat. She remembered Grammy telling of how goat's milk was much superior to cow's milk for folks with queasy stomachs. If Caleb didn't have a queasy stomach, he was doing much better than her. She was able to buy some, provided she would do the milking. That proved to be quite a task.

Kate Flannigan, with her adventuresome spirit, agreed to help. First they made a bed for Caleb in the shade out of harm's way. The escapade would require some elbow room...or, as it turned out, butting room.

The nanny obviously was used to men in britches, for when a gust of wind caught at Kate's voluminous skirt, the goat lowered her head and gave the woman a sturdy thump on the thigh. After a few more attempts to approach in the normal manner, the women regrouped to discuss new strategy.

"It's clear," said a laughing Kate, "that we are going to have to trick the clever little beast."

"Agreed," Tressie said. "What do you have in mind?"

"Well, she has four sharp little hooves, and I don't relish being kicked by them. She has a hard head as well, and as far as I can tell, a good set of teeth. The milk faucets are well placed underneath for their own protection. We have to decide which one of us will do the milking, and the other will simply have to overpower the old girl and hold her down."

Tilting her attractive head, Kate studied the goat, who swayed on spread legs, head down but with her devil's eyes alert.

"Do you suppose," Kate went on, "that the milk will come out if she's lying down?"

"We used to milk cows down home in Missouri, and it never occurred to me to turn one upside down. But I'd wager it wouldn't be a good idea. I think we just need to be real gentle and talk her into letting us have some."

"You can look at those eyes and suggest such a thing?" Kate took a few steps and saw that the goat was watching her.

She dragged in a huge sigh. "Okay. I'll subdue the thing, you get the milk out."

Without waiting for a reply, Kate launched a mighty leap and put an armlock around the confused nanny's neck. Wrestling her to the ground, Kate panted, "Okay, bring the bucket. She's going to behave now, aren't you, sweetie?"

Tressie laughed so hard at the sight of Kate's upturned fanny, her splayed legs, and the goat's frantic bleats that she was momentarily unable to move.

"Might I suggest," Sir Harry said at Tressie's elbow, "that you find something to feed the poor frightened animal, and she'll no doubt let you have all the milk you want."

Wondering why she herself hadn't thought of that, Tressie turned to see the portly gentleman holding out a pan of dried corn.

"Would you two mind doing something?" Kate squalled, one arm around the nanny's neck. "If I turn loose, she's gonna get me."

Eyes rolling, the animal had scrambled to her feet and was putting up a rather impressive tug-of- war, though her poor tongue hung out of her mouth.

"You're choking her. Let her go, Kate," Tressie called.

"More than glad to," Kate replied, and did so.

The goat tumbled to her rear end, then staggered to her feet and eyed all three with obvious hate. A tremulous cry fell from her quivering lips, or what looked like lips to Tressie. She couldn't be real sure.

"I don't blame you, dear," Tressie cooed, and held out the pan of corn.

With one golden eye on Kate, whom she'd obviously settled on as the harbinger of all her troubles, the little nanny sidled up to the corn. Once she had buried her nose in it, all was forgiven and Tressie was able to milk her with no further incident.

Caleb slept through the entire incident, and as it turned out didn't really appreciate the effort. While Kate went to wash up from having rolled around in the dust with a goat, Tressie settled on a boulder in the shade to feed Caleb. Before offering him the milk, she removed all his clothing. Poor little fellow had developed a heat rash under his arms and in the backs of his knees. Fresh air would be good for him. With a feeling of great accomplishment, she gave him the bottle of goat's milk. Caleb was a voracious eater, and at first he slurped away with vigor. Suddenly a look of wonder, then disgust wrinkled his little features and he spat out the nipple.

"Come on, sweetheart, it's good," Tressie said, and again tried to get him to take the bottle.

He tongued it away and set up a howl.

Tressie leaned down close and began to croon to the baby. Her clear young voice rang like bells in the mountain air. Caleb grew quiet and watched her intently. He was such a darling child. Tressie ran the tips of her fingers over his delicate features. How much like Reed he was. She knew those were the Indian features, but couldn't help admiring in the child what she admired in the man.

As Tressie continued to sing the lullaby she remembered from her own childhood, Caleb formed a delighted O with his little lips and his eyes drifted closed. Tressie offered the nipple once again and he began to suck without opening his eyes. Her mind hundreds of miles away in a log cabin in the Missouri Ozarks, Tressie cradled the child, bars of afternoon sunlight caressing his copper skin.

She thought of her own mother and her childhood, so brief and so enduring. Those memories would live in her dreams forever, and now she had a child to share them with. For those brief restful moments, she thought not of Papa's betrayal or that of Reed Bannon.

She had buried her own dear sweet Mama, but the devotion passed to Tressie so lovingly during her own childhood flowed from her heart to encircle the tiny Indian baby. Tressie felt its strength as she had felt no other. Some ties, she knew, were never meant to be broken, and so they were as strong as the very earth itself. As durable as the mountains, as the trees, as the sky and the water. As lasting as eternity.

"I love you, Caleb, I love you," she crooned, bending to kiss the soft little cheek. With surprise she watched a warm tear fall there. She was crying for the first time from joy rather than sorrow, and how wonderfully cleansing it felt. "I love you, Caleb, I love you," she repeated like the words of a song.

The gold mining settlement called Virginia City was on the verge of one of the greatest explosions a community could experience. The cry of "Gold!" echoed all across the mountains reaching out from the Far West in California and tumbling down the mudbound trails. Virginia City had become another Comstock, beckoning even the Forty-niners from that fabled strike. Those with enough gumption who weren't afraid of hard work would make a fortune there in the next decade.

On arrival, Tressie knew little of the excitement. She was utterly exhausted, too tired even to be relieved that the grueling trip was over. She had no more than climbed from the stage than she had an immediate urge to flee the absolute tumult that greeted her.

Clapboard structures grew everywhere, and a great throng of humanity rushed to and fro as if on a commonly shared and death-defying mission. Men shouted and shoved and pushed each other. They laughed and whistled at their animals. Whips cracked, and horses whinnied.

Kate Flanningan's husband met her, and though Tressie could see she didn't want to be rude, the woman was so pleased to see Zeke that one thing led to another, and they departed for their new home behind the freight station belonging to the elder Flannigan. The parting message from Kate was, "Come see us when you get settled."

It wasn't exactly that her newfound friend was deserting her to the unknown. The woman simply hadn't been told all of Tressie's circumstances. It was too embarrassing, and so Kate had been led to believe that Tressie, too, had someone meeting her in Virginia City.

She had changed into her only spare dress at the last rest stop. With her small bundle on one arm, Caleb cradled in the other, she stood on the boardwalk and looked around. Diagonally across the street was an establishment with a crude sign announcing *GOLDEN SUN SALOON*. Tressie searched up and down her side of the wide street. What had she expected? Papa holding out his arms in greeting?

Being alone in such a place was extremely frightening for both her and Caleb. He promptly let her know by puckering up his little mouth to protest. She gave him a hug and kiss. What would she do now? Where would she stay until she found a job? There was nothing left of her little hoard of coins. She'd had no bath since leaving Fort Laramie, she was hungry, and she was frightened. How could Reed have done this to her? The longer she stood there, the worse appeared her circumstances. Crude and dirty men eyed her, leering, circling. And her with a babe in arms. No wonder, either. There were very few women on the streets, and most of them looked like the men.

Biting at her lips, Tressie glanced once up and down the boardwalk. Amid the drab and dirty prospectors, she spotted the most beautiful woman she had ever seen. A vivid flower abloom in the rawness of Virginia City. She was clad in a bright yellow full-skirted dress. A matching parasol shaded masses of her blond curls. Appearing to float above the splintery boards, she drew near and caught sight of Tressie. At first she only hesitated, nodded, and went on by. Then she turned, openly inspected both the young woman and her Indian baby, and returned.

Under the scrutiny, Tressie bobbed her head, jostled Caleb to keep him happy, and dropped her chin to keep from staring.

"What's your name, child?" the woman asked. Her lips were painted crimson and she had the bluest of eyes.

"I...I'm Tressie Majors, ma'am."

"My, aren't you a pretty thing?"

Knowing the woman couldn't possibly mean her, Tressie gazed with pride at Caleb. "He sure is. His name is Caleb."

"Oh, my," the woman said with a chuckle. "I meant you, dear, but he is precious, isn't he? I'm Rose Langue, owner of the Golden Sun there." She gestured with the filmy parasol.

A dusty, disreputable old man staggered along the walk and veered toward Tressie, a string of drool hanging from one corner of his mouth. Rose took her arm, pulling her out of the way so that he stumbled off the edge of the boardwalk and fell to his knees in front of the team of standing horses.

"Git yore ass up out of the dirt," the stage driver bellowed, after which he slapped the reins on the horses' backsides and set them to moving with a mighty shout.

The unfortunate old man barely scrabbled out of the way in time to keep from being trampled.

A couple of men riding by on horses set up a banshee howl. Caleb joined them, screwing up his little brown face in the process.

"Oh, sweetheart," Tressie said, and jostled him gently.

"This is no place for a baby, Tressie. Where is your man?"

She had already thought up a story, and gave it now to this beautiful saloon keeper.

She told her concocted story. "He came out to stake his claim and I followed along as soon as the baby was born. We didn't want to miss a chance, and his brother had already found gold. He could only hold the claim for so long, you see."

Rose studied her with pursed lips. "Indians don't usually file claims. In fact, it might not even be legal."

"Oh, my husband's not an Indian." Caught in her lie!

Rose whooped. "Then, honey, there must have been one in the woodpile, 'cause this child sure ain't white."

Tressie jerked away from Rose's hand, still resting on her arm. "Let me go. Leave me be. I have to go now."

"Oh, you mustn't be so quick to anger, child. You'll soon learn that what few women are here just find it natural to mind each other's business. It helps us endure. Well, you'll soon understand. Here, let me take you and—Caleb, is it?— somewhere where you can get cleaned up. Then you can send word to your husband and he can come get you there. You can't just go wandering around the streets. Do you have any money?"

"Yes," Tressie said, jutting her chin at Rose.

"How much?"

Too tired to carry on with the lie, Tressie lowered her head and didn't reply.

"Honey, this is a gold camp, despite its efforts to look like a real town. A girl like you has no business on the street alone. Now, you just come on with me. We can talk some more. You look plumb wore out."

Tressie admitted she was. She could no longer put up any resistance to such an offer, and so followed along like an obedient child. Together the two women dodged in and out of the masses of mankind that had recklessly gathered in the midst of this wilderness.

Dust choked the brazen glare of sunlight, sifting a grimy coat onto her perspiring flesh. She welcomed the cool shadows thrown by a store with a crude sign that read GENERAL MERCANTILE. Caleb kicked and squirmed in her arms, and she felt suddenly and overwhelmingly weary. Like a cloak worn for weeks, exhaustion dragged at her. Even without a mirror she knew what she must look like in her bedraggled dress and hide-bound feet, with hair that hung to her shoulders in lank strings. What did this lovely woman see? This woman with her white teeth and skin as pale as milk. Her jonquil-yellow dress like captured sunlight, must surely be a vision and Tressie asleep and dreaming.

Caleb squirmed and bellowed. Rose waited a moment in the door of the Golden Sun Saloon until Tressie caught up.

"You'll be wanting to feed that little one and get cleaned up. Come with me."

Together they went to a staircase at the back of the cool dark saloon. Tressie paid little attention to her surroundings. It was too difficult to concentrate on dragging one foot, then the other up the steps and hanging on to Caleb. All she wanted was a bath and bed, but would gladly settle for the latter.

Rose chatted amiably as they climbed. "There aren't many women in a gold camp, nor in the territory, for that matter. There's a great demand for young, pretty women like you."

Tressie was too tired to ask for what, or even think about it much. She could only envision taking a bath and sprinkling on some of what this woman wore that smelled so wonderful, then collapsing on a soft bed.

Caleb's squalling dragged her away from the near stupor. "I'll need some milk for the baby."

They had reached the top of the stairs and Rose halted. "You're not nursing him?" Her tone asked what manner of woman this was, but she kept her mouth shut on the criticism.

Tressie stammered, wondering if it wasn't time she told the truth, but was unable to rouse enough energy to do so. "No. I have no milk."

"Then I'll send one of the girls to fetch you some. Do you need anything else?"

Tressie shifted Caleb and gazed morosely at Rose. "He needs diapers and something to wear, but I have no money." Tressie would go without and not ask, but she couldn't let pride force the baby to suffer.

Rose waved the words away with an impatient, white-gloved hand. "Maggie? Maggie, come here," she called toward the landing where a door stood ajar.

A perky dark-haired girl perhaps a year or so older than Tressie poked her head around the jamb. Rose went over to her and they talked for a few minutes, the girl glancing surreptitiously in Tressie's direction. She wore only a black body corset that shoved her tiny breasts high and held up long dark stockings. After a while the girl nodded and disappeared back into the room. Rose directed Tressie to another room along the hall, ushered her inside, and shut the door with a click.

Caleb found a fist and snuffled as he sucked loudly on it.

"My poor little one," Tressie crooned, smoothing the crop of sweaty black hair.

Rose guided her to a lounge covered in red velvet and Tressie couldn't even object that she was dusty before dropping onto it with a great sigh. Immediately she saw the bathtub. It was the most marvelous contrivance she had ever laid eyes on. One end curved into a backrest with blue and gold curlicues. The inside of the tub gleamed like rich cream. It was at least four feet long. How wonderful it would be to lie there up to her chin in hot, soapy water. Never mind the heat or the soap. She would settle for water.

At the very moment she completed the thought, a muscular young man came through the door carrying two large buckets of hot water. Steam rose up around his thick arms. He barely nodded at Tressie, poured the water in the tub, and left. By the time she had unwrapped Caleb and removed his soaked diaper and clothing, the man had the tub half filled.

He left without a word, and Tressie sat there holding her naked baby and staring with longing at the tub. She dared not disrobe. He might come back and find her that way. Besides, no one had told her the bath was for her.

A soft tap on the door ended her ruminating. The girl called Maggie, now wearing a ginger-colored dress, the bust cut as low as the corset she wore beneath it, came in with some parcels and a bottle of warm milk.

"Miss Rose said to tell you she will bring you some clothes before you finish your bath. These things are for the baby." The girl bent over and tickled Caleb's bare belly. "He's a sweetheart, isn't he?"

Tressie smiled.

Caleb kicked and swung his doubled-up fists. What passed for a grin dimpled the fat cheeks. They both laughed. "He's my tough little brown nut," Tressie said with pride.

Maggie pinched Caleb's chin and made baby talk for a minute, then stood up abruptly, as if remembering a pressing chore. "I'll leave. You must be worn out."

Without giving Tressie a chance to thank her, the delicate woman minced from the room, slamming the door behind her. Tressie waited no longer, but peeled out of the soiled dress, kicked it into the corner, gathered Caleb from the red velvet lounge, and took him with his bottle into the tub with her.

The rising steam gave off a sweet fragrance. On a stand near the tub were towels, washcloths, and a bar of pink soap. Tressie leaned back and sank as deeply into the water as she could without submerging Caleb, who sucked greedily on the bulbous rubber nipple. This was heaven. Whatever Rose Langue had in mind would be fine, as long as she and Caleb were sheltered. Tressie was so tired of living on the edge of disaster, she thought she might do anything to be free of want.

She wouldn't think about what the girls here did for a living. That pretty Maggie with her tiny breasts all but bursting full-blown from the neck of her dress. And beautiful Rose. In the back of her mind, she knew what they were. Everything had a price and she expected this luxury was no exception. She ignored the niggling little voice of warning and dreamily lathered the sweet-smelling soap over first her baby, then herself.

Ten

"They call these hurdy-gurdy houses," Rose explained.

She took Tressie's hand and led her down the flight of rough stairs to the room below. "That's because we have dancing girls but no gambling. The men can buy tickets and dance with the girls. They are also expected to purchase drinks for themselves and their partner. Of course, the girls are sometimes willing to, shall we say, consider other favors. That's what the cribs are for, along the back."

Tressie placed her hand on her bare chest and felt the heat of her flush. The dress, loaned by one of Rose's girls, left too much uncovered and she hadn't even wanted to venture from the room. But Rose had been so kind, she simply couldn't be rude to her. Tressie scarcely remembered coming through the saloon the evening before. She eyed it now from the bottom of the steps. Two kerosene chandeliers with multiple globes hung from the high ceiling. A bar ran along one wall just inside the door. At the back, near where she and Rose stood, was a dance floor. At this morning hour, only one couple, a scantily dressed woman and a young fellow in a flannel shirt and baggy pants held up by suspenders, shuffled around on the hardwood floor.

A few men leaned on the mahogany bar. Spittoons were

lined up under the bar, but the floor was badly stained with near misses. A mirror hung behind the bar, flanked by paintings of naked, quite hefty women. The room was very narrow and dark, the only window being in the front wall. It had a red velvet drape pulled to one side and tied to let in a few rays of morning sun. In the corner under the window, an old man slept, his legs splayed out in front and a disreputable hat tilted over his eyes. A white beard lay on his chest like a massive rug.

"Not too fancy," Rose said in an apologetic tone. "Cleaning up after men is easier forgotten than worked at." She shrugged, smiled at Tressie, and took her arm. "It's a living."

Tressie heard the tinkling notes of a piano, and gazed in awe as one of the girls pounded out a lively tune. The shuffling dancers, who had sat down to have drinks, rose and went back to circling the dance floor, this time with more vigor.

"We just moved in a few months ago," Rose assured her. "I'm only just getting started. Hell, this town is fixing to rise from the dirt like a crop of rain-soaked corn. It's gold, Tressie. Gold that's causing it all. And I'm getting my share without ever leaving the comforts of home. These men are desperate for female company, and those that have nuggets and dust will pay anything to get it. You're a pretty little thing, if a bit thin, and you can stay right here, live good like the rest of my girls."

Tressie watched the man on the dance floor cup his partner's bottom in two dirty hands and wiggle his hips to settle her securely into his suggestive gyrations. The girl laughed down in her throat and leaned her head back so that he was looking down the front of her scanty bodice.

"I couldn't do that," Tressie said, and turned away.

Rose tossed her blond curls and laughed. "Of course you can. What's he really getting, anyway? A touch, a feel, and a dance. All for an occasional buck's worth of whiskey for him and his dancing partner. Anything else he'll pay all too dearly for."

"I don't even like whiskey."

"Oh, our girls don't drink whiskey. Theirs is tea or watered-down coffee. But he pays whiskey prices."

Tressie tilted her head to whisper in Rose's ear. "Oh, my goodness. I wouldn't know what to do. I never...I just couldn't...well, I just wouldn't, that's all." The idea of letting total strangers fondle her, do to her what only Reed Bannon had done, was abhorrent. And most especially these filthy men who didn't look like they ever bathed.

Rose studied Tressie a moment with narrowed cornflower-blue eyes. "How old are you, child?"

Tressie had to think a minute. Finally, "I guess I'm going to be eighteen in February," she finally admitted.

"Then stop acting like a child. You're a grown woman with a child. Since I've seen no sign of a man, I'd guess that story to be pure fabrication. So that means there's only a few choices for you out here. You haul their ashes or you take in laundry or you cook in some sweatbox. And end up wed to some worthless pilgrim who works you to death. Here Caleb will have a warm bed and all the attention in the world. He will never want for anything. Maggie already loves him and the other girls will, too."

Tressie didn't bother to explain her earlier lie. "And all I have to do is let these disgusting men do whatever they want to me?"

"They just fumble and poke around. Most times they're too drunk to do much, and are happy for feelies. And they pay in gold, girl. Think, Tressie, think."

Tressie shuddered and nodded. She fingered the fine fabric of the borrowed dress she wore and the glittery combs that held her auburn hair. Such finery tempted her sorely. What did she have to lose but her respect? And suppose one day she found Papa. What would he think? And Reed Bannon, the only man who'd loved her, touched her. No, she couldn't do it! She simply couldn't, no matter the consequences.

Eyes tearing, she shook her head. "No, I can't, ma'am. I just can't do it. We won't starve; I'll find something. Oh, I'll pay you back for what you've done. I'm sorry if you thought—"

Rose sighed and put her arm around Tressie's narrow shoulders. She hated to lose this one, a real beauty who only needed fattening up a little to attract the men like flies to carrion. If it weren't for the little one, Rose thought, she just might have entrapped Tressie after bringing her this far. Instead, she frowned at her own lack of fortitude and guided the young girl back up the stairs. Sometimes you hit color, other times… well, other times you came up empty.

"Never you mind, child. We girls have to stick together. God knows there's few enough of us to stand against all of them. I have a—uh—friend, Jarrad Lincolnshire, who owns a big mining company outside of town. He's needing someone to cook three squares a day for his pilgrims. But Lordy, Tressie, I wish you'd change your mind."

"I won't have to…?"

"Huh-uh, never. Jarred's got daughters your age. He'll see the men leave you be. Get changed so you don't look so inviting and we'll ride out there before business around here gets too brisk. Maggie won't mind keeping an eye on the baby."

They rode to the mine in a fine black buggy with gold and red wheels and a shiny leather seat. Wearing elbow- length gloves of soft deerhide, Rose held the reins of a dainty-footed red mare who pranced and tossed her head proudly. There had been no rain in months, and the mare's hooves kicked up puffs of powdery dust. Rose produced two white lace hankies sprinkled with rosewater to hold over their noses for the dusty ride up the mountain.

The gold mine operations took Tressie's breath away. Coiling up the side of the hill like a giant snake were great wooden troughs. At the top, pivotal nozzles, each manned by two or three miners, spat water against the cliffs. Earth and debris tumbled into the troughs to be washed all the way to the creek bed at the bottom. Tressie guessed that the gold was sorted out by the miners who labored at intervals along the wooden ditches. It was an impressive operation, and certainly beat panning gold on a creek bank.

A log building and massive tent had been erected in a flattened area on the side of the mountain. There, Rose reined in the mare. A grizzled old man took charge of the buggy after helping Rose and Tressie down. Before they took more than a few steps toward the log structure, a veritable skeleton of a man who was at least six and a half feet tall ducked through the door and headed for the women. He greeted Rose with a gigantic bear hug that purely lifted her off her feet.

When she could get her breath, Rose introduced him as Jarrad Lincolnshire. He took Tressie's small hand in his long-fingered one. "So very pleased to meet you, my dear," he said with an accent such as Tressie had never heard. He softened his r's and dropped his h's a bit like the Englishman on the stage, but with a little less harsh inflection. He, like Sir Harry, was obviously a well-bred gentleman. Tressie hadn't expected to find such men on the frontier. To meet up with two in such a short span of time was even more surprising.

She just knew her mouth dropped open when she stammered out her reply. "Uh, yes. Thank you, I mean…"

She couldn't help being such a silly fool as she looked up and up into the man's gaunt features. He had a long jaw with sunken cheeks, wispy silver hair, and the palest blue eyes Tressie had ever seen. A pair of bright red suspenders held up pants that were ash gray with thin black stripes. He wore a white shirt with ruffles down the front and fine leather boots that covered his knees. When Tressie couldn't stop her unashamed gawking, he threw back his head and laughed infectiously.

Rose chided him. "Now, Jarrad, don't make light of the child. She needs work, and knowing you were in dire straits here since Jacob kicked the bucket, I thought maybe she could take his place and cook for the men. I know she looks a mite frail, but take my word for it, she's not. Wait'll you hear her tale—"

Lincolnshire shushed Rose, not letting her finish telling what little Tressie had related during their ride to the mine. "Well, girl, hit on hard times, have you? Can you cook?"

Tressie nodded and continued to stare up at the man.

"And strong. You must be strong. I really prefer a man for this job, Rosie, you must know that." He shrugged his narrow shoulders, took note of Rose's exquisite moue, and went on. "It's hard work and long hours. I suppose one of the men can keep firewood cut for you. Other than that, the whole job falls on you. Stoking the fire, cleaning up after, and the like. You understand?"

"I can cut my own wood, sir," Tressie murmured, feeling totally out of control of this situation. "I have a baby; he'd stay with me." She cast a hard look at Rose, for she would brook no nonsense about Caleb remaining at the Golden Sun in the care of those "loose ladies."

Lincolnshire hooked bony thumbs under the suspenders and rocked on his heels. "And no man. You poor wee thing. How old is the child?"

"Almost a month now. His name is Caleb and he's Sioux Indian," Tressie said, hedging on Caleb's age just a bit while jutting her jaw at him.

"Holy God, child. You lay with one of those savages?"

Tressie glared, tightening her lips. No one must ever know Caleb wasn't hers. She had nightmares about self-righteous women coming to steal him right from her very arms. Or worse yet, a tribe of Sioux sneaking into her room and plucking him from his bed so they could turn him into what Sir Harry called a "bloody savage."

Lincolnshire became distracted suddenly and turned to Rose Langue to lift her pink fingers in one hand. Bending deeply, he touched them to his lips, and the look of tender love that passed over the woman's exquisite features embarrassed Tressie. She gazed all around, not used to such an open show of affection between two people. It was clear that this man's being married and a father of daughters, as Rose had said, made little difference to the Golden Sun's proprietress. She was madly in love with him.

Lincolnshire led them into the huge tent. "This is where the miners take meals, and yonder is where you'll cook."

Tressie's heart lurched. He was going to hire her. Immediately on the heels of that realization came doubt. Could she do the job? She had never cooked for more than four or five at a time, and that with Grammy on one side and Mama on the other.

The mess tent was big as a barn. To take her mind off how many men she would be cooking for, Tressie gazed around. The canvas sides were rolled up in the heat of day, but it was still suffocating inside. At one end were piled sacks of supplies, crates, barrels, and a tremendous cast-iron stove. Logs had been notched together to form a bar between the cooking and dining areas. Crude tables and benches, cut from logs hewn on one side, filled that section. It looked like a hundred men could eat here.

Tressie decided to ask, but hated to interrupt the soft murmurings between her new boss and her new friend. Since Lincolnshire hadn't kicked her out when she told him about Caleb, he would obviously let her keep the baby here with her. That's all that truly mattered.

He finally turned his attention back to his new cook. "I prefer my help to remain on premises except for time off, and ye'll have little of that. Ye have a place to live, little one?" he asked abruptly.

It took a moment for Tressie to realize he was speaking to her, for he had once again focused a gaze of rapture on the blue eyes of his paramour.

She finally stammered out a reply. "No, I—"

"We'll fix you a place behind the kitchen. It'll be warm there come winter."

Rose broke in. "You intend to winter here? I'd venture most plan to leave out and return in the spring. It's not fit for man nor beast in these mountains once the blizzards come."

Lincolnshire chuckled. "We'll not be going out. We're here for the duration. This is a settlement, woman. It's no longer a primitive gold camp. Soon there'll be all manner of businesses in Virginia City. At this very moment we're taking fistfuls of nuggets the size of my big toe from the placers. As long as the water keeps running, we'll work them. Come spring I intend to sink shafts into the mountainside. There's bound to be veins of gold ore as big as my leg beneath this earth."

"Suppose your men won't stay and work the winter?" Rose asked.

"Ah, the most will. It's good pay for the pilgrims who missed out on their own claims. Well, we shall soon see at any rate, shan't we? Meanwhile, little lady"—he addressed Tressie once again—"I'll have you a cot set up. You go with Miss Rose and fetch your things and the child. We'd all fancy us a home-cooked meal this night. That give you time to settle in?"

"Not so fast, Jarrad," Rosie said. "You haven't agreed on wages, and you'd better pay her well."

Again came the magnificent full-blown laugh from the English gentleman. "Or you'll take it out of my hide in other ways?"

Tressie found herself gaping again. How different were these miners than men she had known in Missouri. To say such things right to the face of two ladies. But then, back in the Ozarks, no one would consider Rose Langue a lady.

The two haggled over Tressie's wages until they came to a settlement that sounded to the young woman like more money than she might have seen in a lifetime of farming the prairie soil. And that was every month! Lord, Rose was right. There were better ways than with a pick and shovel to take gold out of these hills.

With high wages came higher prices in this town inaccessible to transportation for nearly half the year. Rose took her shopping to buy badly needed clothing and bedding for herself and the baby and she saw the salary wasn't out of line

In the general store, she fingered the few bolts of fabric piled on hastily constructed shelves. There was little to choose from, and she had no idea if she would have time to make the dresses she would need. She wanted at least two so that she would have one to wear while the other was being washed and dried.

Rose stood beside her, pretty mouth puckered while she draped swatches of fabric under Tressie's chin. More than covering the body was obviously important to the blond beauty. She finally reached a decision.

"This blue looks the best on you. One of my girls, Lissa, is right handy with the needle. We'll take some measurements and she'll sew you up two frocks from this.

"Later there'll be more to choose from. Freight lines will be forming fast, each trying to beat out the other to service these gold camps. And I think Virginia City will grow enormously in the next few years. Why, there may come the day when you'll see Paris fashions on these very streets. Wouldn't that be grand?"

The woman's enthusiasm was catching, and soon Tressie felt lighthearted and hopeful. Perhaps there was a future for her and Caleb here. One day maybe Reed would come, like he promised, and they could be a family. And Papa, what about him? Did he look like the rest of the men out there on the streets, with their stern and grizzled faces and filthy clothing?

Gaiety dashed, Tressie trailed along behind Rose, who carried the bolt of cloth as she picked up items and lay them back down. Rose chattered and she only half paid attention.

There were so many goods here she could scarcely imagine having a need for more.

"A large crate will have to do for Caleb's bed. A cot won't be sufficient to sleep you both." Rose fingered some soft red flannel. "We can cut blankets from this, and here, this bleached muslin will do for his wraps. At least at the camp there will be hot water for you to do a regular wash. Jarrad didn't skimp on hauling in equipment."

"Ma'am," she finally said to Rose. "1 don't understand why you're doing this for me. You don't know me, and I can't ever pay you back for all this. It's too much, just too much."

"Oh, don't be silly," Rose said. "We're too few, we have to stick together. If we don't help one another, then these darned old men will just get the best of us, and we can't. Besides, I'm enjoying it so much. Now, do you see anything else you need?"

Tressie glanced shyly around, afraid to touch any of the geegaws, for fear they would stick to her fingers. She had no need for such pretties, but my, how beautiful they were. A box of ivory combs with stones like diamonds adorning the curved top caught her eye, and she held both hands behind her back to keep from touching them.

Rose saw the look of wonder on Tressie's face and dipped into the box. She came up with a creamy-colored comb with aquamarine stones the color of Tressie's eyes. "Just one pretty won't hurt. My treat," she said with a smile.

"Oh, but I couldn't," Tressie objected, clenching her hands tightly to keep from reaching for the wonderful comb.

"Now, don't take on. Just bring that darling little boy in for me to visit with once in a while, and consider me well paid."

How strange a woman like this could love babies so and do the things she did that were meant only to bring life into the world. And do them for pure enjoyment. To think about the waste made her sad.

A memory of Reed Bannon lowering his mouth to hers made Tressie tremble. Women did what they had to do, she supposed, and she wasted no more time on judging Rose's motives, whatever they might be.

The storekeeper, a cricket of a man with a completely bald head, cut and folded the blue fabric to Rose's specifications and totaled up the items they had piled on the counter. Tressie gasped at the total and watched the man weigh out the gold which Lincolnshire had given her for advance wages. Their purchases took over half of it.

"Don't worry," Rose whispered in her ear. "You'll not want for anything. You'll have plenty to eat, a roof over your head, and a bed. Are you sure you won't change your mind and come back to the Golden Sun with me?" she teased.

"I'm sure," Tressie said solemnly while she watched the storekeeper wrap her purchases in brown paper. "We'll do just fine out at the mine, Caleb and me," she told Rose, and picked up the package. "And besides, all those men, maybe one will have run across...uh...my husband in his travels. He has to be out here somewhere."

Rose gave her such a look of dismay mixed with pity that Tressie turned away, unable to accept the woman's judgment of her actions. Rose certainly didn't know all there was to know, anyway.

Out on the street, dodging through the hustle of humanity, she continued to search the faces. "Wouldn't it be something if he just walked into that tent one day to eat and there I was cooking? Oh, Rose, wouldn't that be wonderful?"

"Oh, sure," Rose muttered. "That'll happen just about the day Jarrad Lincolnshire makes an honest woman of me. Here we are. Throw your stuff in here and wait. I'll go over and fetch Caleb. Those girls of mine have probably spoiled him rotten by now and you won't be able to put up with him. Just wait here."

Tressie climbed into the buggy, caught up by Rose's bitter

words concerning Jarrad. Rose might cherish her lifestyle, but clearly she dreamed of marrying Lincolnshire. How sad that was for all concerned. Not only his wife far across the ocean, but Rose and Jarrad as well. It was clear that the two were terribly fond of each other, but all those other men that Rose allowed to....

Tressie couldn't even let her imagination near that subject. Instead she gazed around with interest.

The town was fit to explode with sights and smells and sounds. Hammering came from every direction as wooden shacks were constructed and privies thrown hastily up behind them. What a sight to see: the actual birthing of a town. Tressie thought she was going to enjoy very much working at the mine up on the side of the hill, where she could look down on this miracle as it took place. There seemed to be little planning, yet spaces were being left between rows of structures. There roads formed, winding around to accommodate more buildings.

One day, Reed Bannon was sure to ride into this town. And he would hear she was at the Lincolnshire mine cooking and come to fetch her and their baby. Tressie sighed and gazed through a veil of tears into the brittle blue September sky.

What a foolish dreamer she had become.

Velda Brotherton writes from her home perched on the side of a mountain against the Ozark National Forest. Branded as *Sexy, Dark and Gritty*, her work embraces the lives of gutsy women and heroes who are strong enough to deserve them. After a stint writing for a New York publisher, she has settled comfortably in with small publishers to produce novels in several genres.

Facebook: Author Velda Brotherton
Twitter: @veldabrotherton
www.veldabrotherton.com

www.ingramcontent.com/pod-product-compliance
Lightning Source LLC
Chambersburg PA
CBHW050944120626
46552CB00001B/362